ID0483892

STRANDED

STRANDED

A STORY OF FRONTIER SURVIVAL

MATTHEW P. MAYO

FIVE STAR
A part of Gale, Cengage Learning

GALE
CENGAGE Learning·

Farmington Hills, Mich • San Francisco • New York • Waterville, Maine
Meriden, Conn • Mason, Ohio • Chicago

GALE
CENGAGE Learning®

LIBRARY OF CONGRESS CATALOGING-IN-PUBLICATION DATA

Names: Mayo, Matthew P., author.
Title: Stranded : a story of frontier survival / Matthew P. Mayo.
Description: First edition. | Waterville, Maine : Five Star Publishing, a part of Cengage Learning, Inc., 2017.
Identifiers: LCCN 2016058125 | ISBN 9781432834043 (hardcover) | ISBN 1432834045 (hardcover)
Subjects: LCSH: Wilderness survival—West (U.S.)—History—19th century—Fiction. | Frontier and pioneer life—West (U.S.)—History—19th century—Fiction. | BISAC: FICTION / Historical. | FICTION / Westerns. | GSAFD: Biographical fiction. | Historical fiction. | Western stories.
Classification: LCC PS3613.A963 S77 2017 | DDC 813/.6—dc23
LC record available at https://lccn.loc.gov/2016058125

First Edition. First Printing: May 2017
Find us on Facebook– https://www.facebook.com/FiveStarCengage
Visit our website– http://www.gale.cengage.com/fivestar/
Contact Five Star™ Publishing at FiveStar@cengage.com

Printed in the United States of America
1 2 3 4 5 6 7 21 20 19 18 17

To two amazing women:
Janette Riker, for never giving up,
and my dear wife, Jennifer,
for the same reason—and so many more.

"Alone, alone, all, all alone,
Alone on a wide wide sea!"
—*The Rime of the Ancient Mariner,*
Samuel Taylor Coleridge (1798)

"Nature, red in tooth and claw."
—*In Memoriam,* Alfred, Lord Tennyson (1850)

"Courage is resistance to fear, mastery of fear—
not absence of fear."
—*Pudd'nhead Wilson,* Mark Twain (1894)

The following account is based on the true story of Janette Riker's struggle to survive the harrowing winter of 1849–1850, stranded and alone in the Northern Rocky Mountains.

PROLOGUE

"You're old . . . why don't you die and get it over with?"

Janey's whispered words hung in the close air of the small room, between her and the old, wrinkled woman in the bed behind her. The girl heard the quiet, grinding gears of the wooden clock on the cold fireplace mantle. Rain peppered the window and a gust of wind rattled the sash before moving on.

She was sure the old lady heard her. Janey had never sounded so mean before. Her mother's voice in her head said, "That's the trouble, Janey. You never think." But it was too late to take it back. She didn't know what made her say such things, did not know how to stop.

Janey's eyes half closed and she smiled. Maybe she didn't want to take it back. After all, before she left for her silly job at the hospital this morning, hadn't her mother nagged her about telling the truth?

Janey stared through the rain-smeared window panes and listened to the wind. She thought about all that had happened to her over the past year. Too much, that's what. This had been the worst ever of her fourteen years—the war in Europe had ruined her life. It all began when her father had shown her that map. Over there, he had said, tapping France.

Over there. Like the song.

All to help people he didn't even know. She told him she didn't want him to go, had begged him to stay. It was too far. He'd never come back to her, she said. But he hadn't changed his mind.

And now he was gone. The telegram said something about him be-

ing lost in action. Janey didn't want to think about what that really meant. But she knew.

She also knew her mother felt as bad as she did. And knowing they had this horrible thing in common made it worse. Janey sighed, then stopped—she was beginning to sound like her mother.

"Janey."

The voice startled the girl. It was not what she expected, but strong and clear, like the old woman's eyes. Janey turned from the window.

Those odd, bright eyes gazed at Janey, eyes that looked as if they belonged to someone Janey's age, not set in a withered face. It was as if the old woman was always about to smile.

"Janey, please do me a favor."

The old woman, Janey's very own great-grandmother, hadn't said five words to Janey in the two weeks she and her mother had been there. Not that Janey had tried talking to her. Why should she? She didn't want to be here any more than the old woman wanted them in her house. They'd been forced to move in, all because of that horrible telegram and the stupid, stupid war.

"What?" The word came out tight, like a finger snap. Janey tried to look as though she didn't care, as if she might ignore the old woman anyway.

"I said I would like you to do me a favor, please."

All the while the old woman wore that half smile, as if she knew something no one else did. A favor? Hadn't she heard what Janey said to her?

The old woman reached a bony hand, like a pink old bird's claw, into the front of her nightgown and lifted a worn brass skeleton key that hung on a thin leather thong around her neck. Janey had not seen it before, but it looked like it had always been there.

"Here, Janey." She slipped it with effort up and over her head, her long white hair gathered in a soft bun. "I would like you to take this key, please." She held her long, bony arm out, the key dangling from it, hanging in the air between them.

Janey stared at the key, eyes wide. It could be a key to anything. This house was full of mysteries, there were rooms she hadn't yet seen. Maybe the old woman was giving her gold, jewels!

Then Janey's eyes narrowed again. Why would she do that? No, she was an old, crazy woman. And I'm stuck with her all day. And the day after that. And the day after that.

"There is a steamer trunk in the attic. This unlocks it."

The old lady continued to hold the key, and still wore that annoying almost-smile.

A trunk in the attic? Anything had to be better than sitting here, watching an old woman who didn't talk, who refused to do them all a favor and die. Older than dirt, that's what Janey's friend, Beatrice Little, had said about her own grandfather. He had lived with Beatrice and her family for a whole year before he finally died one night in his sleep.

Janey smiled. She liked that phrase, "older than dirt." She'd save it for later, for when the old woman was really getting on her nerves.

"Why? What's in it?"

"There is a small bundle, wrapped in pretty beaded cloth."

Janey stared at her for a few seconds more.

"If you would be so kind as to bring it to me."

Janey sighed and reached out, snatching the key. The old woman let her hand drop, laid back against her pillows, and watched Janey. They regarded each other like that for a few seconds, then Janey stomped across the room to the door.

"Bring an oil lamp, dear. It's dark up there."

Janey turned one last time in the doorway, her bottom jaw outthrust, teeth set, her eyes half closed. It was her best angry look, one that drove her mother crazy. As she left the room, Janey said, "I'm not your slave, you know." But she paused passing the kitchen doorway, and with a loud, long sigh retrieved an oil lamp and a couple of wooden matches.

"Dark, ha," she said, walking down the long hallway. Why didn't

the old lady have electricity in the entire house and not just the kitchen? Everyone else in the world had electricity. It was 1917, after all.

Janey mounted the stairs two at a time, wincing as the wood creaked and popped beneath her shoes. In truth, she was only too glad to get out of that stuffy sickroom. She doubted the old bird would last much longer, especially in this nasty weather.

The attic door stood closed above her, at the very top of the stairs. It looked like all the other doors in the house, polished wood the orange-brown of a bold sunset. Janey had yet to go up the narrow stairwell. Her mother said there was nothing much up there but old things, and a window at the gabled end. She'd go up there and find that trunk and open it with the old lady's magic key. Then she'd grab the beaded bundle—probably silly old love letters.

A smile spread over Janey's face. Now there's an idea, *she thought as she climbed the dusty steps.* What if they are love letters? Who's to stop me reading them? The old lady can't walk, not without much help, anyway, and Mother's not here. But I am, and I have the key.

She looked down at the plain, worn brass key in her palm. It almost made her forget what a spooky place the attic promised to be. Almost.

As she stepped upward, one tread at a time, she wondered if maybe the old woman wasn't trying to trap her up there. Janey paused before the narrow door one step above her. She grasped the knob, turned it. The door inched away, swinging inward toward the darkness of the attic.

Janey swallowed, her throat dry. The glass globe of the oil lamp jostled, made a hollow chattering sound. She hugged it closer. She'd made it this far, might as well get the bundle and get out of there. She could read the letters on the stairs. If they were letters at all. She nudged the door open wider, enough for her to pass through, but first she peered in.

14

The attic was brighter than she expected. Directly across from her was a dusty window, square, but set into the wall on end, as if it were a diamond. It was the same window she'd seen when they first arrived at the old woman's house. Janey had liked how it looked, fancy even though it wasn't.

Beneath the window, tucked to one side, sat a dust-covered trunk. Had to be the one. Janey stepped in and looked around. The attic was filled with all sorts of stuff, mostly junk.

She took a deep breath, let it out. "May as well get it over with." She turned her gaze once more toward the trunk, but couldn't help taking in the few other items stuck up there. Really, there wasn't much, now that her eyes had gotten used to the ill-lit space.

The attic smelled of dryness, of old things. She saw dust trapped in dull light from the window. The sky had darkened more and the big tree out front waved its branches as if it were a slow dancer.

A tall brass lamp stood to the left, its cloth shade in tatters, like an old flower not wanting to shed its petals. Closer to her, also on the left, though tucked further under the eaves, an open-top crate of books sat under a thick film of dust. To the right, a wooden drying rack lay on its side like a bony, tired dog. Then there was the trunk.

Janey walked to it, trying to ignore the squeaks and pops of the attic's plank floor. Without breathing, she stuck the key into the dark, glaring keyhole at the top of the trunk's face. Her hand shook slightly. "Silly girl," she whispered, echoing something her mother often said to herself when she made a mistake knitting.

There was resistance inside the mechanism and she squeezed the key firmer between her thumb and forefinger. She was rewarded with a click-click—something deep inside slid into place.

Before lifting the lid, Janey held the rawhide thong a moment, then looped it over her head. She lifted her hair, letting the thin strap rest against her neck. The key settled at the same spot on her chest as on the old lady.

With a quick breath, Janey knelt before the trunk, unlatched two buckles on leather straps, and lifted the lid.

There was so little in there. At the top of the trunk sat a tray covered in paper of delicate blue flowers with three evenly spaced compartments, but they were all empty. She grasped the dividers, lifted out the tray, and set it on the floor. Inside the dark bulk of the trunk, atop a few old, folded cloth items—quilts, maybe—sat the beaded-cloth-wrapped bundle. She lifted it and found it surprisingly heavy. The covering felt like leather, but old and delicate. It reminded Janey of the papery skin on the backs of the old lady's hands and arms.

What did the old lady want with this bundle, anyway? Sure, the beads were pretty. Or maybe had been at one time. Now, though, they were dull, and some had fallen off. The thin threads holding them were frayed and loose. As Janey held the bundle, a small white bead, then a blue one, popped free and rolled along the rough plank floor before finding a crack between boards where they disappeared.

The girl sighed again. Just like an old person, she thought, to want something that was useless. Then she would ask to be propped up in bed. She would hold this thing in her bony, trembling hands and get all wet and blubbery over it, whatever it was.

Janey felt through the soft, supple cloth. What was inside? A book, maybe? Yes, that's what it felt like. A book.

And then, somehow, Janey knew what it was. It was a diary. Maybe the old lady's diary from when she was a girl. Oooh, think of all the juicy details of the old bird's life from what—a hundred years ago? Ha! She could only imagine what it might reveal . . . "I saw a boy today. He was cute . . . for a farmhand. But I didn't dare say anything to him because this is the olden times and we don't do things like that. Maybe someday people will have guts to speak to each other! Until then I'll write silly little girl things in my diary."

Janey snickered at her wicked thoughts. And then she untied the narrow leather wrappings from around the bundle. Three more beads popped free and dropped, despite the care with which she tried to hold it. *The leather covering flopped apart to reveal what she'd thought it might be—a book with plain, brown, hardboard covers. It was thick, though, more than an inch, and measured longer than her hand and nearly twice as wide.*

Janey sat with the book on her lap, resting on the opened leather wrap. She wanted to open the cover, to see what it said, but something told her that if she did, somehow the old lady would know.

Of course she'll know. You've undone the threadbare wrapping. *But Janey knew it was more than that. She knew that reading the book was something that once done could never be undone. And as soon as the thought occurred to her, it was replaced with another— that she was acting silly.*

A tentative smile crept onto her face. Then she heard the little voice, the one she'd been listening to lots lately. It told her, almost in a chant, that she should read the old lady's secret thoughts. Go ahead, *said the voice,* it will be a stitch!

And so, Janey Pendergast opened the old book's cover and began to read.

Thursday, June 14, 1849

Waiting, waiting, waiting. I am dog-tired of waiting. I wish this infernal trip had commenced weeks ago. Once I have set my mind to a thing, I do not like to wait. I prefer to get on with the task, even if it is as big as moving from Missouri to Oregon Territory. But wishing will not speed the plow. I am inclined to believe what Grandpa Barr used to say: "Wish in one hand, mess in t'other, see which fills faster." A poet he was not, but I will say he was usually more right than wrong.

In truth, I am in no hurry to leave this place, the only home Thomas and William and I have ever known. But even if there was a way to call a halt to the trip, I am not sure I would want to. I would never tell the boys that, as they think I am dead-set against this venture. And it does not pay to let your annoying brothers think they understand you.

After so many months, then weeks, then days, it is hardly believable we have come down to a short stack of hours. We are sleeping for the last time in the house my father and mother built themselves with little help from anyone else. They came to this place, Bloomington, Missouri (back when it was still known, and I do not jest, as Box Ankle), as a young couple, newly married, far from their families back east in New York.

Tomorrow, after living here for nearly eighteen years and raising three children on this farm, Papa will move the family forward, taking us farther still from everyone we know. But we will leave one behind, the most important of all. Mama. She will stay here, tended, or rather her grave will be tended, by Cousin Merdin and his young family.

Funny to think he used to pick on me whenever they'd visit for a special occasion, but look at us now. I am fourteen, and he is all grown up, has a wife in Ethel. I know I shouldn't say it but she is a mousy thing, all bony fingers and shoulders, big eyes and pulled-back hair. It's as if she might fall to pieces if she doesn't keep everything about herself held like a fist, so tight the knuckles are white.

Of course, I expect any woman in her shoes would feel pinched, what with Merdin for a husband and those young'uns, a boy and a girl, if you please. Little Elmer and Ethel, the girl being named for her mama (now wouldn't that be confusing?), are two of the most troublesome children I have ever met. They weren't here ten minutes this afternoon when they turned loose all the hens I had spent an hour shooing back into the coop. I needed them in there so I could gather up the six we planned on taking along before we lit out in the morning.

I about swore a blue streak, but kept my teeth tight, especially when those youngsters hugged their skinny mama's skirts and all but dared me to light into them. And I would have, too, bony Ethel or no, but Papa caught my eye across the dooryard and stared me down. He did it as he always does, silent-like in that way he has of saying a whole lot without saying anything at all. He sort of looks down his long nose, lips off to one side as if he is considering a purchase. But it's his eyes that say it all. I laid off them kids and went about gathering the hens. And all the while Ethel's cooing and hugging *her* varmints because she thinks the chickens gave them a fright.

Those twins are playing her like a tight-strung violin. Good luck on the farm, I say.

I see I am stomping a path around the real reason I wanted to write in my new journal tonight, but all I can think of is how sad we will be come morning when we leave this place behind, when we leave Mama behind. For the life of me I cannot see how Papa will be able to do it.

I asked him that two weeks ago when I brought him hot cornbread and cold spring water out to the stone wall marking our south field from Mr. Tilden's. Papa saw me and waved. Then he finished cultivating the row, and guided Clem on over.

Clem, our old mule, stood off by the thinnest excuse for a tree the farm has, a whip of alder barely eight feet tall, where there was good tree shade not but a few steps away along the wall. As Papa says, Clem never was much for thinking things through. As he approached, one of that mule's long ears flicked, waggling at a pesky bluebottle. I was about to ask Papa if there would be bluebottles out in Oregon, but he looked tired, too tired and sweaty to answer fool questions from me.

Papa wiped his eyes with his shirtsleeve, then slowly, like he was a hundred years old, he lowered himself to a patch of grass on the shady side of the wall. He sighed, his eyes closed as if he was napping.

I swear I wasn't going to ask him a thing, only sit beside him while he chewed the cornbread—Mama's recipe. It made me feel so proud that he liked my cooking, even said it was getting close to Mama's. Now that was a compliment I could take all day long.

Then Papa cleared his throat and looked at me. "Janette, it is too late, I know, but I want to tell you I am sorry for putting you through what we are about to do. The trip west and all."

This caught me by surprise. I could not bear Papa apologizing to me. I don't recall hearing him apologize to anyone, ever. I started to say something but he held up a big, knuckled hand between us, as if to say, "Whoa now."

There were the dark nubs of his calluses, that bandolier of a white scar running across his palm, the visible trace of a bad cut he'd gotten from a fouled plow line years before. I held my peace, wondering what I'd said to make him say such a thing. I felt about ready to crack in a thousand pieces and scatter in a stiff Missouri breeze.

"I have talked for a long time about moving westward, but never really asked your opinion of the trip, nor of your brothers." He smiled and the white lines by his eyes, what he called his "squintin' wrinkles," disappeared for a moment. Even with the wrinkles, he looked younger when he smiled. Maybe everybody looks younger when they smile.

"So tell me, girl." He crossed his long legs. "What is your opinion of the venture?" He popped cornbread into his mouth and looked at me while he chewed.

All I could think of to say was that I doubted the boys wanted anything more than to travel west to Oregon. I unwrapped the tea towel I'd swaddled around the cornbread. It was still warm and moist under my hand. Even on a sticky day, warm cornbread is a welcome thing, one of those little mysteries of life, as Mama used to call them.

Papa accepted another square, held it in one of his knobby hands in his lap. He looked at me with his blue-gray eyes. "That isn't exactly what I asked, now is it?" I could tell he was serious because he kept that sly smile tamped down.

I looked at my bare feet, all grimy around the edges, dusted on top like they'd been powder-puffed. They were dirty enough that they didn't much look like they belonged on my body. "No sir."

Then I gave him that hard stare right back. "Won't it be about impossible for you to leave this place . . . and Mama . . . behind?" I regretted saying it near as soon as it jumped out of my mouth. I am prone to saying a thing that's bothering me, then worry about it too late. But that is the way I am and I cannot do a thing about it.

Papa sat quiet, then sort of leaked out a sigh. His eyes looked tired. "Your mama and me, we built this place with nothing much more than our hands, a few tools—a spade, whipsaw, and my double-bit axe. And one old horse, Clem's mama." He cut his eyes to the sad-looking affair that was Clem, baking in the sun, the row cultivator not moving an inch.

"Then you children come along and put your own shoulders to the wheel, and that right there is what makes a good farm. It's family." He had changed the course of his answer, which was fine by me. He bit the cornbread, chewed longer than he needed, nodding in time with his chewing. In a low, quiet voice, he said, "I will regret not being able to visit with her in the family plot."

He looked up at me again. "But she's not there, you see? I won't really be leaving her behind, because she'll be where she's always been, since that first day I met her at your grandfather's smithy shop when I was fifteen and she was thirteen." He closed his eyes and rapped his thumb against his sweat-dried shirt, the one that used to be blue. "She's been right here in my heart since that day and she will never budge from there. She will make the trip with us."

We sat like that a while longer, then as if told to, we both smacked our hands on our knees to stand. And that set us to laughing. We are so much alike, even more so than the boys are to him. At least that's what I like to think. I know it's childish, but I cannot help it. It's my way and that is that.

I shook the tea towel of crumbs and hefted the water jug. Before I turned to walk back to the house, I asked him the real question I'd wanted to ask for a long time. "Why is it we're going west, Papa?"

"Why? Seems to me we've talked that one to death, Janette girl."

"We've talked around it some, that's true."

He nodded, got that crinkly look around his eyes again. "It's what your mama called my wanderlust."

"What's that?" I asked it even though I had a good idea of what it was.

"Oh . . ." He stretched wide and I heard his shoulders and back pop and crack. "I have an incurable desire to always know what's over the next hill, and around the next bend in the road." He smiled and looked at me. "I expect it will be the death of me one day."

"Don't say that, Papa."

"Oh, I'm only funnin' you, girl. Now you best get back to the house. Do me a favor and make sure those boys are still working on those fence posts. You have my permission to give them what for if they are lazing on their backsides—like me!"

I had to laugh at that, as Papa is the least lazy person you will ever find.

Despite what he told me, I cannot help but think that come tomorrow, wanderlust or no, leaving this place will be a whole lot harder for Papa than it will be for me or the boys.

MONDAY, JUNE 18, 1849

Four days into our trip and I can see that keeping this journal will be more of an effort than I imagined. Not that I am one to shy from effort, mind you. Who else would keep house for these three? That in itself is ordeal enough.

I do not wish to slip into the ease that I expect jotting a list of the day's undertakings can be. That would be nothing but tedious for me to write and for someone someday to read. Which makes me wonder why keep a journal at all? I expect it is to remind myself of the journey one day when I am an old wrinkled crone with my grandbabies about me. If not for that reason, I ask again, why keep a diary?

Yes, every day I do most of the same things "on the trail," as Papa insists on calling this adventure, as I did at home. I cook, I mend torn shirts and trousers, I gather firewood, then chop it for the fire (Thomas is not dependable). I clean and clean again everything we have brought with us. There is that much dust. I haul water when Thomas forgets, or more likely plain shirks the tasks that Papa has set out for him. I also tend the few chickens we brought with us, and I milk our Jersey cow, Floss.

Sadly, she has begun to show sign of strain, even this early in our travels. I think her old udder, swinging low as it is and slapping against her legs, must be a mighty sore thing by the time we stop each night. She walked plenty in the pasture at home, but at her own poke-along pace. She was not forced to walk all day, every day, even if we are not moving nearly as fast as I expected we would.

Papa says he is considering selling Floss at the next prosperous-looking farm we come upon. He says he does not want to have to resort to the inevitable. What that is he would not say, despite Thomas's wheedling, but I think it does not need explaining. And I think it is kind of Papa to think of Floss's comfort, even though he will miss fresh milk and butter. I am the one who milks her and makes the butter, though I was pleased to find the thumping and jiggling of the trail nearly does the churning in the cream pail for me. I will miss old Floss most of all. Her quiet ways and big brown eyes are a comfort. I can write no more of her now, so sad does it make me.

Don't let me sully these crisp new pages with talk of the shame of laundry day. The things I am forced to clean! Young men are, well, I was going to write that they are pigs. But every pig we've ever kept has always struck me as tidy about itself. They will do their personal business in the same spot, usually a corner, so as not to soil the rest of a pen. No, young men are not pigs, but what they are, I have found nothing quite so nasty to compare yet. Perhaps there will be some bizarre beast we'll find on the trail that will remind me of them. On second thought, I hope not, as I don't know how many more sloppy, lazy, messy, rude critters I can take.

This is as good a moment as any to talk of my family. Thomas, my youngest brother, is two years my junior, which makes him twelve. While I am the middle child of the three of us, William, at age sixteen, sometimes seems older than Papa. I do not claim to know why this is, but I can say that he has always been this way, even as a child. That doesn't mean he's the cleanest person you'll find on a farm, but compared with Thomas, I will allow as how William is somewhat tidy.

But there is no one like Thomas. I admit I have not met a whole lot of people in my life, but with Thomas, you get an uneven mix of good and rascal, of laziness and kindness. And that mix changes with the sun. He is without doubt the most frustrating person I know. He still tugs my hair though he has been told too many times to count by Papa and me and even William not to do it. It is as if he cannot resist, as if some devil pokes him in the ear when he walks by me.

Why once, back home, he sneaked up on me while I had a pan of hot bread balanced in one hand and my apron balled in the other, trying to shut the oven door. I spun on him, and smacked him hard on the cheek. His eyes went wide and I remember feeling awful about it, and thinking I had slapped a baby, so innocent did he seem. Five seconds later he was giggling as he ran out the front door. I reckoned I should have whacked him harder.

I am not certain I will do justice to this journal, untouched by my mother, something an aunt from Boston, Miss Minnie, I believe it was, had mailed to her years ago. I recall Papa saying it arrived a month after Mama's birthday, but judging from the inscription it was intended as a birthday gift. Papa said Mama was puzzled by it at first, as the aunt had rarely shown an interest in her during her entire life to that point.

But once she got a leg over that confusion and shock, Mama laughed at the gift. Especially, said Papa, considering the old woman had spent years disapproving of Mama's side of the family and their choices to move away from Boston to New York. Imagine what the old bird would think of us taking the trail to Oregon!

Papa and I had a laugh about that when he gave me the journal. He said Mama had never used it, but he had seen her a time or two with it open before her on the worktable. It would have been of an afternoon when her kitchen chores were in hand, at least for a time. There is never really free time in a kitchen, as something is always needing to be done and you cannot depend on a boy to do a lick of it, asked or no.

Papa said Mama could never bring herself to write in it. She told him it was so pretty and full of possibility that she didn't dare set pen to it for fear that anything she might put in there would sully the beauty of the blank page before her. That was just like her.

He'd laughed at that, but not to her face. He never laughed at Mama. Then he gave me the journal. Said I was to do with it as I saw fit, but that he was certain Mama would want me to have it.

He has told me many times that I am a whole lot like Mama. I will take that as a compliment, though I will also be quick to say, at least here in these pages, that I am a whole lot like Papa, too. And it's that part of me that couldn't wait to commence filling these pages with my words, good, bad, or otherwise.

This journal will be what I make of it. No better, no worse. I am writing small because I have been told I can be windy when I get on a roll. I expect there will be long stretches on the trail when there won't be anyone but Papa and my mule-headed brother, Thomas, to talk with. William doesn't count because he rarely opens his mouth except to eat.

It will be such times I will want to talk to my journal, and in that way I reckon I will be talking to Mama, too. And since I expect I will be the only person to ever read this, I might as well fill it chock-full with everything I can think of saying. And then some.

Now the firelight is low, Papa is dozing sitting up, and the boys have gone to sleep. Papa is being polite and waiting up for me to finish off whatever it is I am doing in this journal. So with that I say good night.

Saturday, June 23, 1849

I have known for some time about the horrors that can happen to people traveling west by wagon. I have read all the guides Papa purchased or borrowed, as well as the newspaper accounts he has managed to accumulate. He is a great one for newspapers, is Papa. There are all manner of atrocities hinted at in those words. Mostly, it seems, they are committed against women and girls, in particular. And mostly by "red savages." By which I am quite sure the writer means Indians.

I do not doubt there is some kernel of truth buried in those lines of type, but I wonder why those journalists need to make out like people should not be told the details. They say such things as "took the utmost liberties" and "committed unspeakable acts" and "bothered in the night." This is not helpful. I for one would appreciate knowing exactly what I am in for should the "red savages" upset our little rolling home. I do not like feather-headed behavior and despise it in the written word. So I will endeavor to fill these pages with the bald truth. Knowing me, that should not be much of a labor.

WEDNESDAY, JULY 11, 1849

We are stopped in low country, a hot and foul place Papa calls "the oven." Actually it is somewhere in the Dacotahs. Same thing as an oven, as far as I am concerned. Why, I do not doubt I could bake a loaf of bread right on the wagon's tailgate as we roll along. Except that loaf would bounce off and burn to a cinder on this foul, scorching ground.

We have been making poor time. Bub and Bib, our oxen, are moving slow and Papa isn't switching on them much. I am glad of it, as you can hear them breathing hard with each step.

Papa has taken to defending his decision to outfit our wagon with one brace of oxen rather than two. When I brought up the topic, he said, "Fewer beasts of burden will reduce our days of burden to all the fewer." I suspect he does not believe that. But it is neither here nor there since we are far from home with no hope of procuring a second brace, nor reversing our journey, not that anyone among us would, save for Bib and Bub.

Papa says he would like to change the way we do things and travel by night, if he can figure out how to make sure the route won't lead us over a cliff.

Problem is, here in these Dacotahs, every now and again we come upon great ravines like cracks in the earth you will see after a rain when the sun comes out and jags up the mud something fierce. Only these cracks are big enough to swallow up everyone in Missouri and then some. No warning, just "blup" and there they are.

I think we should keep moving during the day, no matter how hot it is. I cannot stand the thought of walking on solid ground one minute then stepping off into nothing the next, only to land a hundred feet down, all broke up and not able to do a thing while snakes and lizards and only God knows what else tuck into me like I am a Sunday meal.

We will be staying here today as the heat has taken the steam out of the oxen. A rest is in order, except it is so hot no one will do much more than sweat. Papa and Tom and Will have gone off early this morning to scare up a mess of game, as Papa says. What that likely means is Will and Papa will hunt and Thomas will not be allowed to fire his gun. Still too young, Papa says.

Thomas says that's not fair because when William was his age he was providing for the table for a year or more, and on his own, too. Papa tells Thomas to hold his horses, that life on the trail is different. But really it's because Papa doesn't trust Thomas with a gun yet, I know it. We all do, though no one says as much. Can't say as I blame Papa, but I do feel bad for Thomas. Still, he ought to work harder at pleasing Papa instead of sneaking biscuits when he thinks no one can see him.

There wasn't much more I could do but watch them leave. There went Papa, thin gray hair trailing out from under his brown felt slouch hat, his neck canted forward, reminding me of a turtle I'd seen years before. I always think of him that way—a turtle-looking sort of man. But as if he were the kindliest turtle who'd ever lived. And he is. The kindliest man I've ever known, that is. Not really like a turtle.

As I watched, I noticed that Thomas and William both hold their heads the same way as Papa. Their necks leaned forward, their hats nudged back on their foreheads. Even their hair has that wispy look, Will's the color of browned leather, Tom's darker but not quite black, more like swampy slough water.

And their shoulders—all three hold them the same way,

pulled back but slumped, too, as if they are tugged by strings like on the marionettes I saw at the fair a few years back.

Seeing their hair waving like that in the sweltering day makes me think of when Mama was alive, cooking for us and singing over the stove. She'd open that oven door and heat from the firebox would rush out and blow the stray strands of her hair. Her cheeks red as fall apples, sweat shining on her forehead, her hazel eyes—Papa says I have the same—bright and kind, her mouth always smiling. Always.

And then the fever came. Typhus, Papa said. I did not understand then, and in truth I still do not. I am holding a grudge against God and I don't care who knows it. Papa said it happened for a reason, but I don't think he believes that any more than I do. Anyways, if there is a reason for it, I'd surely like to know of it. No sign yet, but I am still waiting. I reckon it being God and all that I can wait. Time I've got.

But there it was, one day Mama was gone. Papa didn't talk on it very much. Still doesn't. He cried, and right in front of me, too. That surprised me, for I had never seen Papa cry. Had never seen him do much of anything but smile, sweat, grit his teeth, sometimes be a little bit angry with Thomas or the mule, but mostly be my happy, smiling Papa.

After Mama died he became old. For the better part of two years he stopped smiling all the time, didn't much laugh anymore, his hair grew long. It turned gray like the feathers of that old goose we had who honked and hissed and not much else, his old feeble wings dragging their tips, his leathery feet squishing through his own greasy leavings. And then he got better, especially after he decided we were to head west. Papa, not the goose.

The goose ended up stewing on the stove for a full two days, then we ate his stringy old self. He wasn't any more pleasant between my teeth than he had been honking and flapping at me all over the yard. I am certain there's a lesson nested in there somewhere, but I don't have the patience to dig it up.

As they were leaving this morning, Papa gave me one last smile and a quick wave, sort of sheepish-like. I watched the back of his head, my brothers, too, as they all strode, long-legged, into this hot-as-hell wild place that surrounds us.

Papa is hoping to scare up a few rabbits. I have my doubts that anything worth eating lives in the Dacotahs, but I smile and wave and set to work on the baking before the day really hots up.

I would not say so to Papa, but this trip is proving to be a trial.

Thursday, July 19, 1849

Once again it is near dark as I write this by the light of the campfire. I have tried to use my own sleepiness and the fire's scant glow to keep my jottings brief, but I am nothing if not chatty. It is fast becoming obvious to me I will use up all my ink and pencils, to say nothing of my journal pages, long before I run out of events to write about.

Of course the biggest daily worry—not to mention the oxen going lame or one of us taking ill or stepping on a sleeping snake and getting bit as a thank-you—is running out of burning goods. All day long we are to be on the scout for rare lengths of wood or pats of buffalo dung. The dung, I have come to learn, does not stink when it burns, as I had feared. It also does not throw much smoke, and offers a mild, even heat. When we find dried dung pats, we toss them under the wagon, onto a canvas hung underneath the belly of the wagon like a lazy-day hammock.

Were it not for the dung pats, some of them still not firm in the middle, and I blame Thomas for gathering those, I would be tempted to ride in that swaying hammock. Along about the middle of these hot afternoons, when the sun is pinned high and cooking everything like a grasshopper on a hot coal, that looks like a most comfortable spot. But then I commence to thinking of poor Bub and Bib and how hard they are working to lug all our possessions. Why, it's all I can do to not beg Papa to turn them loose and hitch me and the boys in the harnesses for a spell.

Of course I know that's foolishness, but it will do my heart good to see Oregon, for a lot of reasons, one of them so the oxen can recover from this journey. I cannot imagine being born into life as a beast of burden.

If we can't lay a hand on much of anything that might feed a fire during the day, then that night we are reliant on our store of wood and dried dung, but using those scant stocks is a slippery slope. For if we go too many days without adding to the stores, we eat hardtack and jerky. When we are in an area with little to offer in the way of burning goods, we make our fires small and kept alive only as long as the food requires warming.

We were cautious, but somehow the jerked, smoked venison stores depleted more rapidly than Papa had expected, such that they were nearly gone by the time we reached the Dacotahs. And the reason for it still makes me shake my head. Here is what happened. . . .

Once in a great moon, I have seen Papa exhausted, his patience sorely tested, his jaw muscles bunched so tight I bet he could crack butternuts between his teeth. But nothing like that day, not long since, when he caught Thomas with his hand in the jerky pouch. It's a leather affair lined with oilcloth, two brass buckles holding it closed. It rides tucked inside the rear-most of the wagon, back at the tailgate where we keep goods we use most frequently, namely the cooking setup. I knew we were about to see something none of us had ever witnessed. It was Thomas who received the full brunt of Papa's unexpected rage.

Papa's timing could not have been more perfect, nor could Thomas's be any worse. By the way he had gone about squirreling his way into the pouch, tucked away out of sight as it was, it was obvious Thomas had been filching the jerky for some time.

"You!" Papa's voice boomed, startling even the oxen, a mighty task in itself.

Thomas tried to jerk his hand away—I saw it all as I was handling the lines, steering the oxen. We do this while walking beside them. We all walk, for the most part, as the wagon has but a thin seat and Bib and Bub have enough to do without hauling our sorry hides, along with everything else.

That being said, Papa asks that I ride now and again. He insists it is so the oxen will not forget the importance of being driven by a proper seated driver. He is full of beans, of course, and being kind to me as the only girl. I pretend to take offense to this, but secretly my feet enjoy the rest. I ride now and again for a few minutes to humor him. I expect Thomas wouldn't mind a ride now and again, though. And to that I say, "Ha ha."

Working the lines takes little effort, as the oxen are not particularly clever, but they are solid and will keep on churning long after a draft horse has quit its task. Papa says the only thing worth more is a brace of mules. That's neither here nor there, especially as we have no mules.

I was alongside the head of the wagon, a position I was quite familiar with. It was the middle of the afternoon, after I'd swapped with Thomas. That must have been when he indulged each day. No one saw him because he was lagging behind as he usually did, or so we thought.

We had been warned by Papa and his many guidebooks that layabouts and thieves on the trail could not be tolerated and if captured should be dealt hard justice. From the number of such mentions, it sounded as if shirking and thievery are ways of life once one takes to the westward trail. In truth, I think it is because of the slow-witted ways of so many folks.

I have heard tell of people, mostly children, who tumbled from their wagons or snagged on the brake lever and got themselves run over for their careless ways. I also read of others who were foolish enough to allow their families to get so far ahead they were beyond shouting distance, and so they were soon forgotten and lost on the trail!

What happened to them has only been guessed on, but that is the worst of it, I think. The mind—at least mine does—plays the game of terror. I think up such foul circumstances for those lost laggards. And since it is only in my mind, and now on this page, I say to them, "You ought to have stepped livelier!"

And then, in my mind, snakes and wolves and lions and red-skinned Indians all set upon the lost souls in their various evil ways. I could go on but it is a gruesome occupation and I have other things to tell.

This had been Papa's concern, I have no doubt, when he looked back and didn't happen to see Thomas walking along behind, grudgingly stretching his legs mile after mile. I saw Papa drop back from his usual spot alongside Bub, the left ox. It was not odd for him to do so, and we rolled slowly onward, that right-front wheel hub still squawking as though it is a bairn in need of mother's milk. Papa continues to grease it, but he told us we had best get used to it, as there is little more he can do.

Next thing, I heard his shouting, louder than that squawking hub. I yarned on the lines and halted those beasts as quick as they are able. It takes a while for the words "Whoa, now!" to travel from my mouth to their brains, which I suspect are the size of dried peas. That may be mean of me, but a fact is still a fact.

William and I looked at each other, our eyebrows high, in that blink of time before you find out what something means. All we knew was that Papa was shouting, which hardly ever happens, and he was out of sight, and so was Thomas. As I mentioned, Papa had been preaching to us all along the trail about how people are run over by their own wagon wheels with more frequency than you might imagine.

I set the brake and by the time I had looped the lines, then pulled these ragged skirts of mine to step lively, Will was already back there. He has always run like a startled rabbit. Though I suspect Thomas is getting faster.

Even if I had been riding in the wagon, I would not have seen through because I had washing and blankets hung inside every which way, hoping to get them dry enough to take down before we got back into a dusty stretch.

And there was Papa. He is a tall man, and his long finger poked down less than an inch from Thomas's face. Thomas was backed up real good, there being nowhere else for him to go. He'd shrunk himself up into his clothing like a turtle skinnying into his shell.

But it didn't do any good, because Papa leaned right into him. As soon as Will and I got there, we saw why Papa was riled. Thomas was pinned by Papa in such a way that his guilty hand was still jammed right into that satchel of venison. He couldn't have moved it if he wanted to. And I bet he wanted to.

None of us had ever seen Papa so worked up, not since Mama passed, anyway. And then it was grief, not so much anger. Though when someone dies, you are most certainly angry, now that I reflect on that. But who can tell me who it is you should be angry with? Is it God? That doesn't feel like the right answer, at least the Bible thumpers would not have it so. But if not God, then who?

That is something I can mull over later. As I was saying, Papa repeated his word, as if for our benefit, though I doubt he was aware Will and I were standing next to him. The veins in his sunburnt neck stuck right out and reached all the way up the side of his face under his hat. His eyes were narrowed and fiery and his jaw set tight, trembling. He shouted that one word again: "You!"

Will put a hand out to touch Papa's sleeve, but I stayed it. It was too soon, and as I had not seen Papa in such a state I was a little afraid of him, I will admit, though he had never given any of us cause to feel that way.

Will pulled back as if he agreed with me. Then slowly Papa's jaw muscles softened, those veins throbbed less on his neck. Finally his long leathery arm, so muscled it looked wrapped in rope, slowly lowered, his pointing finger curling inward.

No one made a sound. Up front, one of the oxen shook his head at a blowfly and his dull neck bell clunked.

Papa turned, pulled in a deep, long breath, and ran his hands down his face as if he was washing. Then he let out his breath like it was a long, slow release of pent-up steam. Without turning, he spoke in a voice that sounded as if his throat was sore. "We cannot stand greed on this trip, Thomas. It brings harm to us all."

Thomas shifted, and in a whisper said, "Yes, Papa. I'm . . ."

But Papa held up a big knuckled hand and Thomas kept his peace. Thomas is prone to go on and on if allowed. I am one to talk. I have used up too many precious diary pages already relating this incident. But I will say one more thing. Papa stood like that for some time, doing something he has been doing more and more lately on our journey.

He looked eastward, toward where we had come from, and though I did not want to disturb him, I looked at his eyes and saw things that I have yet to experience and hope I never do. I may be bold and foolish in my guesses, but I fancy I saw regret and guilt and sadness and worry and fear all at once in those eyes. It wasn't until that very moment that I began to understand what Papa was thinking, the load on his two wide shoulders has to be so much more than we know.

TUESDAY, JULY 24, 1849

I vowed early on in this endeavor that if I had little more to say in these clean pages of paper than to tally the day's chores and travails (often one and the same), I would leave off writing here. And that is what I have done, at least until I have something of note to tell. Today is not one of those days.

And judging from the slow, dusty progress we are making, it is unlikely that tomorrow, or any day on the horizon, will offer much worth relating. This is not a complaint (well, perhaps a little of it is), so much as it is a fact.

And so we roll slowly toward Oregon and what Papa is certain are its farming splendors. I hope it proves greener than this worrying, hot, and dusty land we find ourselves trapped in.

With that said, I doubt I shall write again here for some time to come. It occurred to me that I should use these pages more wisely, spend them like hard-earned pennies instead of treating them as if they numbered as many as snowflakes that fall in a midwinter storm. It is hot enough here, somewhere in the Dacotahs, that I tempt myself with thoughts of the cooling snows of winter. And still I fill the pages! Will I never learn?

MONDAY, AUGUST 20, 1849

As I promised myself in this book close to a month back, I have kept from writing here until I have something to say. Today is that day, as we caught sight of far-off peaks, those of the Great Rocky Mountains. Long have I read about them, and when we spied them I turned away, pretended the dust was too much in my eyes lest Thomas poke fun of me.

Gripped by whimsy, Papa smiled and said, "Won't be long now, my dears. We are within spitting distance!"

Whereupon Thomas promptly up and spit, paying no heed to the stiff breeze that had accompanied us all the day long. His spittle whipped back and caught him in the eye. Even William shook his head. I fancy he smiled, too. I know I did.

The notion of those majestic peaks has abided so long in my mind I had grown fearful that on seeing them they would somehow appear as diminished versions of those I think about. But no, even from this great distance—Papa says we are the better part of a week from them—what I can see of them speaks of boldness. So much so they made me weep.

I will admit that here, but nowhere else. And now, as that bit of foolishness has passed, I will mention it no more. The Territory of Oregon may well be our destination, but it is the Great Rocky Mountain chain for which my heart sings.

SATURDAY, SEPTEMBER 22, 1849

On reading my last entry, I decided to keep from writing for a spell, as I would offer more of the same frippery, waxing about the mountains. So I forced myself to leave off until we grew close enough to the mountains that I might relate my honest impression of them.

And so I shall, for we are here, at the very foot of the mountains I so longed to see. With that arrival, in as pretty a little grassed valley as you could ever imagine in all your days, came a sudden stretch of work, accounting for my inattention to these pages.

Papa says we will be here but three days. He minced no words in telling us he fears staying put longer, though the spot is pretty. He says the winters here in the mountains come early and stay late. He could not help but look quickly at me when he said this, and I take that to mean he knows I am aware of what he speaks.

This is true, as we have both read the same guidebooks (William cares not for reading and Thomas is too flighty in the head to settle down with a book). More than one of those guides warned against lingering too long on this side of the great mountains in the latter days of September and into October.

This is something I worry about more and more as we roll westward. I spoke with Papa about it once, some weeks ago, and he was oddly gruff, telling me we would have ample time to make our escape. Then he excused himself from the fire, attended to his evening duties off in the sage somewhere, and retired to his bedroll.

The truth is, I believe I was correct. It pains me to say it because if he were ever to read this I would be mortified. But we should have left Missouri sooner than the middle of June. We also should have traveled faster, and with other wagons. But as we are now here, and as Oregon, near as I can figure, is to the west of these mountains, I am confident we will be fine.

Papa says he and William and Thomas will spend one day hunting buffalo not far from here. He says we would be foolish to neglect the opportunity to replenish our food stocks while we can.

Also, Bub and Bib are as lean as a pair of bone-rack oxen can be. Papa swears this grass will fatten them enough for the last pull up and over these stunning mountains. The grass looks sparse and on the verge of browning all over, but the oxen, once hobbled and turned loose, appear quite content to graze it down.

I see once again I have nibbled at these pages without saying much. The firelight is low, I am tired, and there is much to do tomorrow. I will leave off for now.

SUNDAY, SEPTEMBER 23, 1849

The tomorrow I mentioned last night came and went, busy as I expected. I find myself alone in camp as the sun drops away, the first time that has happened. I am not particularly worried, as I know Papa and the boys are off hunting for meat we will need to continue the journey. And hunting is, as Papa says, mostly luck, with a little dumb luck tossed in for good measure. That aside, I had a big day myself. I am not tired and there is much to relate, and so I shall, while the day's light is still with me.

It began, as all our days do, at the campfire. I fed them up big for their day of hunting, and packed biscuits and dried fruit for them to take, besides. Papa sent the boys off to get themselves ready, while he lingered at the fire, his hands wrapped around a cup of hot coffee. Rarely will you find a man who enjoys his coffee as much as Papa.

"Now, Janette," he said. "We will do our best to make it back here by dark. It will depend on the buffalo. But I have seen much good sign these past several days, so I am inclined to believe we will have good luck." Papa leaned closer to me and winked, "But it wouldn't hurt if you were to wish us luck, maybe say a little prayer."

"I can do that, Papa. I was going to anyway."

"That's my girl." He searched around himself as if he'd misplaced his hat again, patted his coat's front pockets. "Now, where did I put that rifle?"

I could not help but smile at him. He'd leaned the rifle against the wagon, within arm's reach. I looked over toward the gun, pointed with my head.

He followed my gaze. "Ah ha, now Janette, what would I do without you?"

I said what I always say when he asks that, the same thing I've said since I was a little one. "You'll never have to worry about that, now, will you, Papa?"

"Girl, I am happy to hear that." The thing he always says. It is one of many habits of conversation he and I get up to. I don't think he does the same with the boys, but I am not sure what sort of talk they get up to when they are out hunting or working together in the fields. I want to know, but only because I am jealous of the time they get to spend with him. Why, I thought for the hundred-and-tenth time, did I have to be born a girl?

"Remember, Janette, keep that scattergun nearby, you understand? There is a handful of shells, enough to do the job. Keep them dry, and close to hand. I mean it, keep that gun close. I don't like leaving you here but I can't very well take you and the boys, and I trust you more than them to hold down the fort, keep the fires burning." He winked at me again. I knew he said that last bit to help me feel better about being left behind. And I reckon it helped a little, but not for long.

"I'd leave one of the boys here, but that would be Thomas and I know he'd be underfoot. And besides, I'll need that young horse to carry back all the meat we'll be making."

"It's all right, Papa. I understand."

Papa stared at me then. "Nearly fifteen now, is it?" He shook his head, his worried eyes relaxing, the sides of his eyes wrinkling like they do when he smiles. "You are the vision of your sainted mama, save for your dark hair where your mama's was corn-silk gold. But make no mistake, you are your mama's daughter."

"I am your daughter, too, Papa."

He acted as if he hadn't heard me, and kept shaking his head.

"And kindly like she was. You're nearly her age when we were married. Can't believe it's been six years since we lost her."

He got that cloudy look again, his smile faded, and a little morning breeze pushed those stray strands of gray-white hair around his cheeks. He looked very old to me then, looked older every day, if I have to be honest about it. And I always try to be honest about such things.

I reckon life on the trail will do that to a body, day in and day out, walking the whole way, working the switch in the air over the backs of the oxen, teasing then onward, westward toward Oregon. We hear nothing but the grating of the iron wheels over the never-ending rock and jagged rubble, rolling too hard down washes, barely making it up the other side again, Papa yelling for us to not get behind the wagon lest the oxen falter and roll backward.

But the grinding wagon wheels and hubs screaming for grease aren't the only things that make noise in the wagon. Utensils and tools rattle and smack every time we drop back down hard off a rock or roll into a rut. I was a fool to think we could somehow manage to keep from breaking Mama's four prize teacups. I did manage that very thing, every one of them.

Well, there is one last cup that, though chipped, still looks like a cup and not a handful of jagged pieces of cup. I have vowed to myself and to Mama that I will protect that cup and use it once we get to Oregon Territory. It rides in the very middle of my clothing, cushioned by stockings and underthings.

Papa has not told me so, but I do believe in my heart of hearts that he has grown bone tired of the journey west. Might be he didn't want to light out in the first place, but Papa has never been one for changing his mind once a course is set. I think all the planning gathered speed like a train chugging downslope, then got ahead of him, out of his grasp, rolling faster and faster. And then he up and sold our home place to Cousin Merdin, and that was that.

Now here we are, much of the way to Oregon, with the most difficult stretch still to come, a long leg of the journey over mountain passes that will require us all to be as sharp as knives. But I don't see that keen edge in Papa's eyes. I have not seen it in a long time, if I am honest about it.

As if he were reading my mind, I caught Papa staring east again, toward Missouri. "I thought it would be worth it. All that fertile farm land the pastor's brother wrote of. I almost wish that rascal had not sent those letters. Maybe if I had not read those accounts by them who have already made this confounded trip . . ."

I'm not certain he meant for me to hear that. It was almost as if he was speaking to himself and did not know I was there, my ears working.

Then he smiled and pulled in a deep breath and straightened his six-foot-tall frame. "Your mama would be so proud to see you now."

"And the boys," I said, in my best mother-hen voice.

"Yes, yes," he said. He looked over his shoulder at my two brothers, Thomas poking and punching at William, William gathering gear and trying to ignore Thomas. "But those lads, they're different. They're not like you."

"I hope not," I said. "They're boys!"

That got a laugh out of him, then William said, "Pa—"

But Thomas shouted over him. "I expect if we don't leave soon we'll miss our chance to find a buffalo today!"

They watched Papa as he poked at the cookfire, sparks spiraling up into the pale early sky. Papa winked at me and pretended he'd not heard them. This was almost as fun as a stage play.

Thomas was still tugging on his second boot. He'd snugged

his hat so tight onto his head it mashed his ears out. I try to get him to go easy on his poor ears, but he has always been that way, in a hurry and no cares at all but for what is right in front of him. Sometimes he reminds me of a dog. I really will have to let him be.

Papa kissed me on the forehead, grabbed up his rifle, and walked past the boys. "I am on my way to find buffalo. What are you two laggards going to do all day?"

William pushed away from the wagon where he'd been leaning and fell in line, with Thomas bolting after like a spring colt, stumbling forward on his long legs and pushing on William to edge him out of the way.

"Bye bye, Janette!" shouted Thomas, and William, like Papa, only waved, already intent on the task ahead.

"Goodbye! Goodbye!" I shouted, waving and smiling. "Bring me back a buffalo robe!"

I watched them a moment more, my hand above my eyes as if I were saluting them. Really I was blocking the sun warming in from my left, up high like a sizzling egg in a vast blue pan. It is odd to me that such a cold night as we had could be scooted out of the way by such a warming thing.

Papa and the boys disappeared from my view for a moment and I felt a sudden coldness in my gut. Then there they were again, lined side by side, nearly perfect, along a ridge of bone-like rock, hard and gray and unforgiving. They waved to me and one of them, I wager it was Thomas, shouted something, but I could not make out the words. Whatever he said was carried off, broke apart like old, crumbling tree bark gone powdery in a breeze.

They waved big, wide exaggerated waves, funning me, I know, and I was tempted to shout back something, anything to them, but for once I had no notion of what to say. Why is that? I waved, the same as what they gave me, a foolish long thing that

I kept up long after they stepped down the other side of that rocky ridge and out of my sight. I dropped my left hand from my salute and walked the few yards back to camp.

I collected the tin breakfast plates, feeling a whole lot more than my usual twinge of jealousy of the boys and their time with Papa. Now and again I still resent being a girl, though over the past couple of years I have grown somewhat used to the idea, regarding it less like a punishment and more as something I am stuck with that must be endured.

I have also come to realize that women are stronger than men. And I do not say that lightly, for Papa is a strong man in most all ways. But how else could I cope with all that needed doing around camp while they hunt for buffalo? Then they will bring it back with them and I will have to cook it.

I prodded the low coals with a stick, got down on my knees with my skirts bunched in one hand, and blew on the coals to revive them. In short order, steam rose off the washing-up water. And then it came to me—this would be the only time since we took to the trail back in June in Missouri that I would be alone, well and truly alone. I felt a zing of excitement along my backbone.

Three months, it had been. Three long months with little time to be alone, never really out of sight of any of them. I smiled and rubbed my hands on my apron. A new and exciting feeling bubbled in me as if I had been given some surprise gift, all wrapped and tied with ribbon. It could be anything! The day could bring about anything at all.

With a tin cup of weak coffee in one hand, I stood and looked around me at the little valley Papa had chosen for us to rest up in. There were Bub and Bib, hobbled and noses down in the sparse green grasses, their jaws working away at what must have tasted as good as hard candy to me.

"Eat up," I said, nodding toward the oxen. "Who knows what

those mountains yonder will bring." They ignored me. I did the same to them and faced the mountains to our west full on. They were tall and not far away.

Rocky arms, like broad wings, all but closed in the valley. A quick gust of cold air chilled me then. Pretty as it is, I will be glad to leave this place once we have dealt with the buffalo meat.

In the meantime, I do not feel guilty one bit about having all this time alone, all to me, and no one else. It's like a birthday feeling. "I will relish this day of solitude." I said it out loud. My fancy words had no effect on any living thing within earshot— the only ones I could see, anyway, them being Bub and Bib. They kept eating grass.

I do not know what I expected, but the birthday feeling had already begun to pinch out. I did my best to kindle it up again. There I was, all alone and faced with a pretty day. I had chores to tend to, of course, but there wasn't enough of those to worry about. They wouldn't take the entire day.

That's when the two Janettes in my head commenced to bickering. There was the one who wanted to lie on that big boulder close by the wagon and nap in the sun like a lazy barn cat.

Then there was the Janette who frets on everything. She felt sure Papa and the boys would find their buffalo soon and be back before I knew it. Somehow she always wins. She told me that surely this would be a good day to get a leg up and over the baking.

So I let myself sigh long and loud and figured if I worked steady until midday, I could have enough biscuits and loaves for a few days, anyway. The way the boys ate, it wouldn't take long for them to look at me as if I was starving them. Since they were out there making meat, as Papa said hunting was called, I reckoned it would be shameful of me to spend the day doing what I wanted.

And then there was the washing, something I hatefully admitted my time would be better spent on. Having the river at hand was a boon I could not ignore. It would make my life easier to do the washing with all that fresh water so close. And without Papa and the boys underfoot.

I sighed again for good measure and set to the tasks, trying and not succeeding in the least to not feel resentful. Papa was one thing, but the boys are doing the only thing I have longed to do for months now, which is to see something, anything, beyond this endless trail.

And it's only because they are boys and I am a girl. They get to do the things I loved doing back home in Missouri. Wander through the woods, see what I could see beyond those jagged mountain peaks. No matter how close we get they keep themselves out of reach, even though we have been rolling toward them for weeks.

I did my best to tamp down the raw, bitter feeling I let bubble up inside me. It wasn't doing me any good. And it certainly wasn't getting any work done. I dragged the big washtub off its hooks on the side of the wagon, and set it by the fire. Then I slid the bails of the water buckets onto the hooks of the shoulder yoke and lifted it onto the back of my neck. I lugged the entire swinging affair down to the water's edge.

I got close, and while I looked for an easy path, I commenced to slide down the bank, but stopped myself with the help of a big tree root. It is bent like a person's leg and poking from the riverbank, perfect as you please, right where I wanted it.

The washing took longer than I expected, but mostly because I stopped more than I ought, keeping a sharp eye toward the southwest, where they had gone. Not that I wished them back so soon, but I did expect to hear the boom of Papa's rifle. This land is a big place, and they likely had to walk far to find buffalo, deer, any sort of game. But as much of this land is not treed, the sound of such a forceful gun should carry on the wind.

Early in the afternoon a cold breeze out of the west filled the wagon canvas, slapping and whipping it like a banner. I know by now not to cinch the ends tight because the wind works it harder, like a rooster fighting his own reflection in a puddle—no matter what, he will not win. So I let the breeze carry on through. I hoped it might cart off some of the smells of food and the boys and wood smoke. I let it blow and continued with the washing. By my estimation we still had three or so hours of sunlight when I finally finished.

I figured my next chore should be to gather more firewood, at least enough for another day, since Papa said we will be here for three days, then move on through the pass. In truth, it doesn't look like much of a pass to me, and I almost said so to Papa when we first arrived, but I held my tongue.

As if he was reading my thoughts, Papa had winked at me, said not to worry, he'd scout it. I thought maybe they'd inspect it this morning, but the pass, if it is one, sets west of the wagon tongue. Which is north of where they headed. I will ask him about it tonight.

Big winters in the mountains, Papa had said. Indeed, and with today's wind, I believe it. The air has already taken on a cold touch, like a kiss from the dead.

As the washing dried on my zigzag of rope lines, and the bedding aired and sunned on the big rock I had wished to nap on, I gave in to my laziness. I sat down and sipped hot mint tea and reread one of Papa's newspapers. As I have said, he and I are the only ones who enjoy the written word. William now and again will indulge in a few pages of the Good Book, but he soon closes the cover and seeks distraction elsewhere. Thomas . . . I do not know about that boy. I know he can read, but I do not know how he learned, so fidgety is he. Me, I read for the pictures

I see in my head.

Some writers, notably the newspapermen, I have found, have such a way with how they put together all those words that I find myself not minding much that I reread them, time and again. Even if some of those writers are featherbrained in their thinking and too fancy with their descriptions. They can talk and talk about a thing and never get to the point. That behavior galls me, though I fear I am prone to it in these pages.

I don't have much other choice, as we are limited in our materials. There is a small but solid selection of newspapers, two guidebooks for emigrants heading west to Oregon, both with surprisingly little useful information about our chosen route. And of course, the Riker family Bible, much of which I know by heart.

Even if the Bible's words sound good, I admit that much of their meaning hasn't come to me yet. I have faith that if I keep on reading it, someday it will all make sense. I hope so, anyway. I have spent far too long with that big book on my lap to miss out on any secrets it may have for me. I harbor a fear that I will one day realize it isn't any deeper a well than I have already discovered, and that the water I have sipped from it is all I will get. Time will tell. For now, I remain thirsty.

I had finished rereading the first few pages of *The Emigrants' Guide to Oregon and California* by Lansford Hastings, when I heard a noise behind me. I would like to say that being in Indian country I have grown bold enough that I made a grab for the shotgun first thing. But no, in these pages I will tell no lie.

I admit the first thing I did was to mark my spot on the page with a finger and look up, squinting at the waning day's sun, off to the west. I still did not see anyone walking toward camp, weighted down by humps and tongues—the tastiest cuts of a buffalo, as we have come to learn.

I decided to take out this journal and catch up on my

thoughts and events, such as I have any that are worth relating. And that is what I have done, for many pages now, I see. I hear the sound again. I mark my place on this page and look up.

It is only the hobbled oxen clunking their great curved horns together as they graze close by one another. I am still alone and the wind is growing colder.

Sunday, September 23, 1849

It is later the same day, or rather it is night once more. I write this by the light of the fire, but it is difficult to see the page. I could use a second fire behind me. I have noticed that campfires are all too much in one direction, not enough in another. Sort of like Mrs. Devalaris back home. She could be your best friend when she needed something, but once she got it from you, in my case help with her preserves last autumn, then you would be lucky to drag a hello from her tight-lipped self.

I decided she was a most unpleasant woman. I told Papa as much one dark afternoon while I was baking, and he said it was not her fault, likely she was dropped on her head as a baby.

I had checked the bread for the last time, knowing it was near done, when I stopped what I was doing and looked over at him. He was sitting at the kitchen table with his big hands wrapped around a cup of coffee. It had been cold early that fall and Papa liked to have a cup of something hot before he went back out to milk Bess.

He kept his face straight, so at first I did not know what to think of his comment, then he couldn't help it and a laugh popped right out of his mouth.

It was made funnier if you know Papa never likes to say anything bad about other folks. But I guess Mrs. Devalaris and her fickle ways even got to him.

But that is about enough of why our old neighbor is like a campfire. I am cold and there is no sign nor sound of Papa and the boys. I should say I am not terribly alarmed, as I can picture them holed up, huddled around their own warming blaze, hands held out toward it, while thick slices of buffalo meat sizzle on green sticks.

It has only been one day, but I would give a lot right now to have them back here with me. I will admit it is frightening to be alone like this. I don't much like it, but will have to put up with it, probably until morning because only a fool would try to walk back through these strange woods in the night to get back to camp. And Papa is no fool. Nor is William. But Thomas . . . he will likely be a fool a while longer, anyway. I hope he outgrows it.

Still, I will keep the fire burning all night long, I vow it.

MONDAY, SEPTEMBER 24, 1849

I did as I said I would on this page but hours since: I kept the fire going all night, and now I am woefully low on a supply of wood. But I see plenty of down trees into the woods at the edge of this meadow. It is daylight and I cannot wait here in camp doing next to nothing. It is foolish of me, I know, but I feel as though I have to go look for them. But if I should leave, Papa and the boys might come back when I am gone.

Would they worry about me? Would they think I went missing while scouting for them? Or worse, would they think something awful happened to me? That thought bothers me most of all. I am in a pickle.

It is several hours later, judging by the sun. I take it to be nine to ten o'clock in the morning. They are still not back here, so I have written a note to them, folded it once, and set it where they cannot miss it—on top of the stewpot's lid. If I know the boys at all, they will beeline for the food. I did not bother to reheat the stew. It is no longer chunks of potato and carrot and onion. It is now mushy soup, but will still taste good to them when they return.

Much of another hour has passed and there is nothing for it, I am nearly out of my skin with worry, so I will go on the scout for them. If I do not meet up with them after an hour of straight walking in the direction they left, I will turn back. I still have plenty of hours of daylight left to me. If I am feeling bold and confident of my direction, I will take a different route back to the camp, so as to cover more ground.

Tuesday, September 25, 1849

It is the next day and I will tell you what happened to me yesterday. I made an adventure of it—and I wish I had not. I am the most foolish young lady to ever have lived. I am convinced of that. Here is what happened:

I reached what I perceived to be the limits of a safe distance from camp, a distance I daren't exceed, I told myself. And then I kept going. That is the way with me. I cannot tell myself to do a thing, for then I become affronted and go against my own grain.

Would that I could change who I am, but I suspect that would be like asking a crow to please take up swimming instead of flying. I did retrace my steps, but only partway down off that ridge top. Then I cut northeastward, intending to come upon the valley from the southern edge of the river.

I felt sure I should know it when I saw it because the valley we are camped in is the only wide, flat stretch for some time along the river. It is a brambly, rocky path with barely room enough on the narrow trail we took to get here with the wagon.

I was most pleased I brought biscuits with me. I had been so worried that I had not eaten anything, and only tasted but a few swallows of water before I set out hours before. I reckoned I had made it halfway back to the camp when I began to feel weak inside and out, and not because I found no sign of Papa or the boys.

I tried at one point to convince myself that fresh-snapped

branches about knee-height (for Papa, anyway) were signs left by them. But I also saw hoofprints of deer in a patch of soft ground where I expected to see boot prints.

I cannot allow myself to believe in things that I know are not true. I bit the inside of my cheek to keep from crying and sinking to my knees right there in the dirt. Instead I stayed my course, and continued walking.

I kept a spire of rock in sight that I'd seen from camp. I knew it was northeast of the wagon. I reckoned if I aimed for that I would have to make my way to the left of it once I got down near the river, and that should put me somewhere near the camp. Getting lost out here would do nobody any good, least of all Papa and the boys should they find I went missing once they made it back to camp.

The path I carved wasn't all that difficult since there's more rock than tree out here along the boney spine of this mountain range. The trees tend to grow in patches, with big stretches of gray, slidey rock between, though without order to anything at all. Papa told me to be careful any time I was to find myself near rocks, especially those with crevices in them, and notably along sunny mountainsides. He had been told of the number of snakes living out here, and early on in our journey made sure to tell me and the boys all about them.

Rattlesnakes. We'd had them back home, of course, but he told us time and again they were nothing like out here. Cold weather would be easier since they tended to den up, but as it isn't all that cold yet, I stepped slow and cautious.

I tell you, I was some glad to get down off that rocky slope and away from any danger of late-season snakes. I know they are looking for a few more hours of sunlight before they curl up for a long sleep. Soon enough, however, snakes became the least of my concerns, as I realized I had made a poor choice in what direction I took to get back to the wagon.

By the time I made it to the river, it was coming on darker than I wanted it to be. I could still see, but everything around me was taking on shadows and nothing looked familiar. I had no candles nor lantern with me, only the hope that the thin curve of moon I'd seen the night before would offer help. But it was clouding right quick, and when I looked up to get a fix on the rocky spire, I got a surprise instead. The fool thing was not there.

I had come too far down along the river to see it. That rock was somewhere out there, hiding behind the trees. I should have known I might well miss it. I must be more intelligent about such things. My abiding thought was that Papa would not be impressed when I stumbled into camp long after dark.

Mostly, though, I had hoped to see a snapping, dancing fire across the river to guide me over. I still had gray light from the skies, and I took full opportunity of it.

The river gave me fits. Try as I might I could find no place to cross to keep from soaking through. I roved the bank, but it didn't work. Soon I gave it up for a bad job and stepped down off a snot-slick rock straight into the freezing water.

My skirts bunched in my mittened hand, my satchel held high in the other. All day I'd regretted not lugging the shotgun with me, but now I was glad I didn't have to hoist it over my head with one hand. I don't think I could have done it, so heavy is that old gun.

My breath was the first thing to be stripped from me. Never have I felt anything so hot and cold all at once. Jagged icy teeth bit right into me. It was as if I'd been stuffed inside a freezing fire. That might not make much sense, but trust me, it was cold as cold can be.

I finally righted myself. As the upstream side of me was slammed by the water, I fought to stay on my feet with each sliding step. The jumble of rocks beneath me made it a task like no other and I still couldn't raise a decent breath up out of my throat. It came in stutters, as if I was on the edge of a sneeze the whole time.

The water hit me higher, but there was nothing for it, I had to keep moving. When I thought I might have to turn around, the water looked to be shallowing, which meant I was gaining, so I plowed on ahead.

Through it all, the day's light was fast leaving me. I had to make it to the other side quick, so I could get to camp. Hopefully Papa and the boys were there, not worried about me yet, and with a giant blaze licking skyward.

I am convinced it was the thought of Papa and the boys that saved me. That vision kept me dragging and stumbling toward the north edge of that river. I made it to the muddy bank and jammed a wad of skirt betwixt my teeth. This freed up a hand to grab a rock or a root, so I might hoist myself onto land. If I let go the skirts, long as they are, they would tangle around my legs and put me in a worse situation.

Though clawed from the cold, my fingers managed to snag a snarl of tree root and I held on with all strength. But the move nearly cost me my footing. I thrashed with my free arm, trying to keep my balance, and caught my mitten top on a branch wagging in the current. I pulled to free my hand, and right before my eyes my sodden mitten peeled off and, along with the flour-sack satchel I'd brought my biscuits in, slipped from me and sucked away down the river. I barely saw them bob and swirl before they were gone.

"No no no!" I shouted, mostly for the mitten, but also because I hate losing anything, especially for foolish reasons. I thrashed in anger, grabbing willy-nilly at roots and dirt and that bobbing, half-submerged branch. I kept my footing through all this nonsense and made my way downstream another ten feet. Of all the good luck a person can have in such a situation, that narrow course pounding off to my right left a sandy rise at the bank that gave me a quick way out of the river.

I hauled myself toward the bank, slopping sink-footed through wet sand. When I got close enough to firmer ground higher up, I dropped to my knees and crawled forward, sucking my left boot free of the muck.

Though I sorely wanted to, I did not rest on the riverbank for long. Light was nearly gone and the night had grown cold. My teeth rattled as if they were musical instruments.

"Papa!" I shouted as soon as I got my feet under me again. I knew they would be off to my left, upstream of me, though how far I was not certain. None of the riverbank looked familiar, which did not mean much since we'd only been there a couple of days. Nonetheless I felt certain I was more of a distance from camp than I hoped.

I staggered forward, stomping feeling into my waterlogged legs, and felt them freeze tighter with each step. I had to make it to our fire soon or I would wake up dead, as Papa has said in jest. The hidden truthfulness of that phrase, however, was enough to keep me moving.

I walked that way for what felt like hours and cursed the clouded sky for its lack of moon glow, all the while shivering so hard I thought I might lose my brimmed hat.

It was by chance that I heard the low, timid bellow of either Bib or Bub, I did not much care which. I suspect the beast was reacting to hearing me. The oxen were hobbled and there was plenty of good grass in the meadow, so I knew I had to be close to the camp.

"Papa?" I shouted that one word half a dozen times, but heard nothing in response. The wagon had to be close by, but where? Maybe the campfire was blocked by a low rise in the land.

At that point I believed Papa and the boys would by then

surely have made it back to camp. Then I walked right into the Dutch oven I'd upended to dry in the sun on a stub of rock, smack between the wagon and the fire ring. Then I knew for certain what I already knew in my growling gut—they had not made it back.

Cold as I was I shouted their names over and over, staggering around the campsite, walking into things, knocking them over. I groped in the dark before me with stiff hands, one wearing a frozen mitten, one bare and red raw. My tears froze on my cheeks and I did not care.

"Papa? Thomas! William!"

Over and over I cried out for them, but no one called back. I did a foolish thing then—it was my day for such behavior. I sat right down in the dirt, somewhere in the dark at the campsite, and kept right on crying.

It is something only babies are prone to, and given that I was close to freezing to death, you think I would know better. It took me a few minutes to get over my foolishness. Since there is no one else but me here, no one to make a fire, no one to dry me out, in time I stopped blubbering and got to work. I reckoned that if I didn't do it, no one else would.

It took me a short while scrabbling on the ground to locate the fire pit. I found it, and in the doing of it, managed to cover myself in soot. Finally I laid a hand on the dry twigs and bark scraps I needed to get a fire started. But I did not bother with making a fire outdoors. I had to get warm and quick. I knew I was in trouble when I stopped shivering. Given how cold I was, I reckoned that not shivering had to be a sign of something going from bad to worse.

I managed to climb into the wagon with my legs behaving as if they were from some other person. Fumbling in the dark, I felt for the door of the tiny sheet-iron stove. I jammed the small bits of burnables into its firebox and added twigs from the bunch I'd set beside the stove the day before.

The sulfur matches, I would use one. Papa says to burn them sparingly, but this was no time for such worry. Where were they? Think, Janette! With the flint and steel. But where was that? I had used it the day before and set it . . . yes! Inside the tin, wrapped in oilcloth, beneath the wagon seat, as Papa kept it. How could I forget such a thing? Realizing I was forgetting things I should know made me more desperate to get the fire lit.

One thing on another, heaped on another still. That is the way life has been since we took to the trail.

But when I opened the tin, there were no matches in sight. We kept a few elsewhere, but I could waste no more time hunting them down. My hands shook terribly, but I grabbed up the flint and steel. It was a mighty effort to strike the steel hard enough to shower off sparks. I am a fair hand at starting a fire, better, I daresay, than Papa, and certainly better than the boys. But not last night. No, the sparks hit the tinder and winked out with no promising glow to follow.

I tried again, and just as I was about to scream in frustration, a single spark caught, nibbled its tiny glowing heart into the edge of a twist of dried grasses. It was one of several such clumps I'd made to help start the stove of a morning.

These I had begun making a month or more back, in the Dacotahs, and Papa had praised me for being clever. In keeping with his annoying self, Thomas made fun of the simple little fire starters.

"Who is laughing now?" I whispered as I blew cautious life on the tiny nest of smoke and flame in the stove. I leaned twigs on top of more twigs with my shaking hands, not caring that smoke clouded my face. My hands were so cold I almost did not feel the growing new warmth. But I could see it, and that was enough to quicken my heart's beating and bring a smile to my face.

I would make a fire, and I would dry myself out, and I would live through this day of mistakes. I cursed myself for straying from camp for those many hours, and for letting the fire die out. What if Papa and the boys had been reliant on the smoke, the sight of flame in the dark to guide them back to camp? Fear and shame and worry warred in me, stabbing my gut with their poisonous barbs.

WEDNESDAY, SEPTEMBER 26, 1849

I awoke in the dark of early morning in the wagon, cold and stiff and sitting upright, my back to the trunk that contains Papa's things. I know what is in it because Papa said he had no secrets from me. I don't think that's true, but it is one of the things people tell each other to let the other person know they trust them. At least that is what I hope that means.

I did not feel badly about going in the trunk while Papa was here, rummaging for something to read or to fetch something he told me to bring him, but now that he is gone, no, now that he has not come back yet, I admit to feeling odd, as if someone is watching me when I go in his trunk.

My teeth ached from the cold, as if I were breathing the dry air that blows off an iced pond. It hurt my throat and nose, but it was so dark I could not see my breath, though I knew it was clouding in front of me. Even under two bonnets and a tight-wrapped scarf my hair felt cold.

That should tell you how very cold it was—so much do I hate bonnets that I vowed long before we set out on this journey that I would only wear a bonnet again if we were to attend a church service. And that has yet to happen.

I shivered terribly, as if my bones would click together like knitting needles, and I listened to the dark, to the still night, afraid to speak. Who was there to speak to? I was afraid if Papa didn't answer when I said something, that meant he and the boys had not yet come home to me. I kept my peace and listened instead.

In the dark I played a game, a silly passing fancy that I was all alone in the whole world, and that if I knew where I was I might never again find the place I should be. That made more sense as a notion in my head than it does written down on this page.

I sat like that, the only sounds tiny cricks and cracks from my small struggling fire, and my own breathing. I thought of Bib and Bub. Where were they? How far away from me in the dark? I thought of Papa and the boys and asked the same questions. How far? How far from me? I knew they had not come back. Else they would have roused me, hugged me. I ache for that.

I don't remember how long I sat in the dark, eyes open but seeing nothing. I slipped into sleep again and when I next awoke the day was coming off bright. Blue sky peeked through a gap in the bunched canvas at the back end of the wagon. I heard the slow clank of the oxen's bells not far off.

"Papa? William? Thomas?"

My words floated in the air. Why weren't they back yet? I knew I should not, but I did the thing Papa always tells us not to do—I panicked. Again. My breath came out in shorter, faster bursts and I felt that tightness in my throat and hotness on my cheeks.

I cannot continue to cry every time a predicament comes up. I bit the inside of my mouth so hard I felt sure I was going to draw blood, and I climbed my way like a stiff old woman out of the wagon. Of course I poked my head out first for sign of anything that wasn't right. I am not sure what I expected, but this is a land of surprises and mysteries to me. I hope Papa and the boys return today so I will never have to know what this place is capable of.

I stood in the new sunlight of early morning. The campsite is not as tidy as when I left yesterday morning. On my return last night I made a mess of everything there is to disrupt. And I do not care. This is no camp without them, so what shall I do about it? I shall tidy quickly, mostly myself, for I am a sooty mess, then I have to set off again.

I do not for a moment trust myself or my own judgment. The mind is an evil trickster, an ill-bred thing at best, but I have little choice. I packed a sack with what is left of our jerky supply, three potatoes I cooked in their jackets in the fire's coals yesterday morning, and the last of the biscuits. I cinched the lot into a canvas sack, my pretty flour-sack satchel now gone wherever rivers take such things. Perhaps someone downstream will make use of it. More than likely it will end up forever snagged in brambles and sticks and mud.

I have decided once more against taking the shotgun with me, as it might slow me down, and I have a burning urge to track them before I lose whatever sign of their trail might be left. I have to know which way they went, beyond where I watched them disappear from my view over that far rise.

Now that I know something of the countryside, I feel certain I will come upon them on the trail. They will be tired, carrying sacks of heavy meat, walking slowly. That is the reason they have not yet returned—they are laden with buffalo meat. I will find them.

Wednesday, September 26, 1849

I am writing this sitting on a rock far south of the camp. I am at the spot where they stood when I last saw them, three days since. They were waving to me from this very ridge. It's a grand view, but I do not care about that right now. I am weary and worried and my eyes burn from squinting at the wide, never-ending land. When I do finally catch sight of them I want to be able to wave them toward camp.

Sunday, September 30, 1849

It has been four days since I last wrote. I have been busy, spending my mornings roving as far as I dare, bettering up my wind and hiking back here well before dark, though it pains me to give up on their trail while there is still light in the sky. I leave earlier each morning to lengthen my hours of searching for them. I also have taken to shouting and I do not care if Indians or lions or bears or snakes hear me. This wicked little valley and the ridges that rise about it echo with my shouts of "Papa! William! Thomas!"

I cannot help myself, even now, as I write this I have stopped to bellow their names.

Bib and Bub do not care. They graze, though the grasses are withered and brown. They nose at them hard and chew deep into the dry dirt for tender rooty stubble. If they are worried they do not show it. The only thing they show is ribs, and that is one thing I can say I share in common with them. We none of us is faring well in that regard.

I would bake them biscuits, but as I have never heard of an ox eating a biscuit, and as I am worried about running low on flour and bread soda, I will leave them be to forage as best they can.

I talk with them, spend time patting and scratching them, but they ignore me and swish their tails as if I am an irksome bluebottle.

I shall spend some of tomorrow's morning hours here at

camp, righting it around and gathering firewood. I have a plan to burn a blaze outside, large enough for the smoke to be seen during the day and for the flames to send a mighty glow at night.

This will take much wood, but what else have I to do? My kin are all, and are lost to me at present. I will do what I must to bring them back.

Monday, October 1, 1849

I awoke to an unwelcome surprise this morning. Snow lay on everything in sight. Even on the oxen's backs. As always, they do not notice. It is little more than a layer of dust that will likely melt off by midday, but this morning I have no regard for it.

Used to be I loved the first snow of the year. But that was a long time ago. Here, in this place, the sight of it chills me to my gut, for it means many things, and none of them good. It means long, cold months ahead, months that Papa had said we would spend in Oregon, which he promised is a warmer place on the other side of these foul raw-rock mountains jutting to heaven nearly all about me.

The snow also means I need to get busy gathering firewood, for if it takes Papa and the boys more time to get back to me, I will need heat and fuel for cooking, and digging wood out from under snow is a task I do not care for.

I am thankful that Papa saw fit to pack his two axes, the smaller one he calls his "limbin' axe," and the large, double-bit brute. I can heft the larger, but it is a trial. I do not like the feeling I get when I hoist it aloft. Having the blade of that thing hanging over my head is an unpleasant sensation. I try my best to give it a high swing like Papa always says you need, so as to get enough power to bite into the wood. Then a picture comes to mind of me dropping it right down on my own head, and I falter.

It reminds me of a mad invention by the French, something

called a guillotine. A foul thing that delivers a slicing blow to the neck and lops off the head of someone who did something offensive to someone else. But honestly, how much worse could it be than to have your head sliced off? Truly, the mind of mankind can be a nasty thing.

That invention haunts my dreams. But then I should consider myself fortunate, as I expect the people whose heads came under that thing are long past dreaming.

I decided today to set that double-bit aside, at least until I can work on getting something more pleasant in my mind than a guillotine. That, and it's so heavy I can barely use the thing for ten minutes before I am tuckered out. The limbing axe is a lighter tool, single-bladed, but it goes dull quicker.

Still, I am getting better at using Papa's stone and keeping an edge on it. It is the same stone he carries in his pocket in the field. He always says to keep an edge on things is the most important part of cutting anything. That's why when he works the fields he'll stop every so often and give that long scythe blade a few licks with the stone. He can use that thing so sweetly it sings as he whisks it along the blade.

I try to remember exactly how he ran the stone over the axe blade, but for the life of me, all I can recall is a circular motion. All those times I've seen Papa swing an axe and sharpen blades and make that stone sing, and all I can dredge up is that he works that rough-smooth stone in a circle.

Then I remember it isn't round and round, but he sort of smoothes it along the blade's edge. I tried that, and while I can't say it sang to me, it did sort of hum. Maybe I am imagining that part.

I am careful to do it right, maybe too careful, because Papa says you can ruin the steel if you do it wrong too much. But I must have done it right, because with the next big branch I tucked into, the blade made a satisfying whapping sound and chips spittled out of there looking like something you'll find near a beaver-chewed tree.

I had to stop and admire them, so proud am I of that sharpening job I did. I kept at it until it felt like I was working harder than I should, and that sort of let me know maybe the blade needed another few licks of the stone. Papa always says that a dull blade will cut you bad, but a sharp blade never will, unless the tool is mishandled.

I will admit when he first told me that I did not understand what he was talking about. I must have shown that on my face because he smiled and stopped me at what I was doing—hatcheting on kindling for the cookstove. This was a few years ago, back at the farm.

"Janette, girl, what I'm on about is that a dull blade is like a . . ." He paused to look around, as if the words he was talking about were waltzing across the barnyard. "There," he said, pointing. "Imagine old Nell there." Nell was our old plow horse at the time—she passed on a good six months or more before we ever left.

I knew she wouldn't have made the journey with us to Oregon, but I let myself think she would have. I could use her sweet company now. She had the prettiest eyes. But I'm all off the track again. What I was talking about was Papa pointing at her as she stood in a sort of daze at the corral gate, watching nothing in particular. "Now imagine her without any teeth."

"Why?" I said. "You know perfectly well Nell has a good set of teeth still, even though she is getting on in years."

"Getting on in years?" said Papa, smiling. "That old horse was around before they ever invented the idea for years!"

"Papa, that's not a nice thing to say about old Nell. She is sweet."

"Yes," he said, nodding. "I'll give you that much, she is a kindly old thing. But what I am on about is that if she didn't have any teeth there would be no way she could chew through that tough hay we feed her. Like a dull blade will skin right off whatever it is you're trying to cut or carve with it. And where does that blade want to end up?"

He looked at me and I did not want to disappoint him, but for the life of me I had no idea what he was on about. I was still thinking of old Nell not having any teeth. I'd about decided I could mush up her food for her when Papa asked his odd question. I shrugged and looked at him.

"Oh, Janette, you have to pay attention now. I won't always be around to teach you the few things I have worth learning, girl." He tugged out his handkerchief and mopped at his sweaty face, lifting his grimy hat enough to dab at his forehead.

"Papa, don't talk such nonsense. You will always be here for me." I smiled.

He got real serious on me then. And I reckoned he was right. Funny, I haven't thought of that conversation we had so long ago, least not until now. And with Papa and the boys wandering around lost in the mountains hereabouts, I wish I hadn't chased that thread today. It has made me sad enough that I don't think I want to write any more this day. I will dream poorly tonight, too, I know it.

It is not even anywhere close to Christmastime on the calendar and already I have read and reread all of Papa's newspapers and manuals, the family Bible, every word, not that I understand them all. There is no way I care to guess what some of those words mean, though there are plenty of others that give up their meaning all too easily.

But I will force myself to think back on that lesson on how to sharpen the axe blade because, as Papa says, there is a time for foolishness and a time for work, and the two best not mix. Now it was time for me to work. I needed the firewood and I didn't need to be reminded of anything except that right then.

I went back to working that blade with the stone and it paid off. The task grew easier with each swing of the axe. I was soon heated up in fine shape. I knew that meant I would have to swap out these damp clothes for dry clothes, but I will have to bathe first.

The thought of it chills me, but I push it out of my mind until I chop enough lengths of wood sufficient to keep me in warmth and cooking fire for two days. And then I drop another dead standing tree, for good measure.

When I say a tree, I am talking of trees that are dry, bark sloughing off, and no bigger around at the base than my leg. They burn well, being dry wood, but they do not offer much heat, being of the softer variety. I have yet to find any heavy, dense trees and suspect this raw country is bereft of them, too, on top of all the other things it does not have.

Still, to be fair, this wood is about all I am able to handle. It is forgiving and easier than a hard wood to chop up. And some of the trees are so dead they don't need felling with an axe. I push on them and they give up the ghost with a satisfying crash.

The topsoil hereabouts is thin enough, all matted and veiny with hairlike roots from smaller, scrubby plants growing low down. They, too, are fairly sparse, and I suspect the roots of the trees do the same thing—spread outward like stretched fingers at the end of an arm. I expect that's because there isn't much in the way of opportunity for those roots to worm their way down into rock. And it most surely is rock I am standing on, if the mountains here are any indication.

I manage to lay low as many of these rattly, easy burners as I can. They are a good twenty to forty feet long. If I am lucky they are easy pullers as well, and have at least the nub of an old branch I can muckle onto and drag behind me. I can do three at once if they're fair to middling. I grab one tucked between my ribs and my right elbow, sort of locked in there. Then I bend low and grab another with my right hand, Then with my left, I hold the handle of the axe, midway down, and hook the axe head around a branch nub. Or if there isn't one, I sink the bottom of the blade lengthwise in the trunk and drag it along behind me.

I am thankful right now that I don't have to go all that far from camp, but I see that this patch of forest, a mix of old and new growth, will not last me for long. I am in great hopes I won't have to range further to find firewood, since I expect we will be away from here soon. But back to the wood, once I drag it to camp I spend time limbing the trees and then set to chopping them into useful lengths. That part is the hardest work, I don't mind saying.

I am blessed to have the wonderful little stove that Papa bought for the wagon. It is a solid sheet-steel beast that glows like a pumpkin when it's been working many long hours. But it takes a lot of wood to get it warm and keep it that way. Were I prone to, I could not sleep for long stretches as the wood burns quickly and the stove's firebox will not hold much at one stuffing.

Nothing from these pines goes to waste. I salvage every scrap, from the wood itself right down to the crumbling sleeves of dry bark, which works exceptionally well to help raise a fire from embers. To this smoking bit, which I blow on to help along, I add twigs from the smallest branches, from out near the tips, then bigger and bigger bits, not very long, as the stove won't stand anything of length.

I snap what I can over my knee, though it is now a bruised thing. Both of them, in fact, but it is a quick method and I will gladly suffer bruises to get the task in hand. When I have had enough bruising, I lay the branches against the jut of gray rock nearby the wagon, and I stomp them. I do not prefer that because those pieces wing up in any direction they choose, like moths on a mission, and sometimes they stick me quick as a gunshot.

I am prattling on and on about firewood, using up precious blank diary pages, and who will care? I am the only one who will read this one day. I will look back on this journal and smile. Maybe even read some out loud to Papa and the boys, perhaps on a grand Sunday afternoon family meal.

We will all be sitting around a long, fine table. Our crockery will be bone china and there will be glass windows on all sides of us. As we talk we will eat good meats and warm biscuits, potatoes, greens from our gardens, perhaps yellow squash and carrot, and green beans. And through those windows I will spy long, rolling fields all planted with wheat and corn and grasses, their tips silvering in a late-summer breeze under a stretch of sky bluer than Mama's eyes.

And above it all the sky will be quilted with enough goose-down clouds to make us smile and guess at shapes. The breeze reaches the full, shiny green leaves of the oak already setting its acorns. There is a white slat fence surrounding a greensward where I can hear children giggling. I cannot see them clearly yet, but I will. One of these evenings as I write this I will let my fancy fly even further along that thought trail, and I don't doubt it will bring me much comfort.

I came to in the midst of that thought and realized I had been standing in the campsite, shivering as the sun traveled to the west behind me. I found myself facing the east, like Papa. I wonder if I am beginning to think as he did. I worry I am letting sorrow into my mind.

TUESDAY, OCTOBER 2, 1849

I have been here all alone now, except for the oxen, for more than a week. I know how many days have passed because I scratch tiny marks, like sticks, on the side of the wagon, in a spot where Papa would not mind seeing them. Four upright stick scratches with one dragged through them, corner to corner, to make it five sticks. Tomorrow I complete a second bundle of stick marks. Today makes nine days I have been alone. I did not count the day they left to hunt.

I know now that they are lost in the wilderness, somewhere out there, in one of the directions I look toward every day, all day. I have lessened my range since my earliest forays out into the surrounding wilds, concentrating instead on building up a goodly supply of firewood and counting and recounting the goods we have in our stores.

If they do not show up soon, I will need to follow suit and go hunting. It is not something I have done much of. But I know I can do it, for I will need food and will have little choice. I eat sparingly, so that when they do return we will have enough of the basic victuals to carry us through the mountains.

How far we are from Oregon I do not know. But it must be some distance yet, since Papa felt it prudent to hunt buffalo to make enough meat to last us through. The thought does not hearten me.

I spend half my days scanning the valley floor to the east and the ridges all around. The other half of the time I curse myself for not doing something, anything to help them. But what is it I can do? I gather more firewood. Perhaps if I keep a fire burning day and night, I will be able to at least guide them back to me.

I move the oxen to spots where they will find more to eat, but those spots are further and further from the wagon. I have considered hitching them and moving the camp, though not far enough away that when Papa and the boys return they would not see me. It is a good enough plan, but I have never hooked the oxen alone. The yoke weighs more than I do—I can barely lift it.

I don't believe Bub or Bib would ever do me harm, but they are big beasts and could hurt me without knowing it. They are becoming irritable and getting them to the river to drink has become a dreaded daily chore. I tried hobbling them close to the river one day, but that night I heard one of them kick up a fuss and in the morning found the bank had given way beneath Bib's great weight. I had to lead him upriver to a low spot where he could climb out.

I keep the camp tidy and contained, not strewing our goods far from the wagon, for fear Papa will return in a hurry and tell me we must move and right away! Such thoughts spark bright inside me.

Leaving in a hurry will be fine with me, for it means Papa is back safe and sound. But it hasn't happened yet. Likely the only direction they could travel was due southwest. It stands to reason they found it near-impossible to retrace their steps. Perhaps the landscape is too steep! It is far easier to climb down a rock face than it is to climb back up it. That means they have to take a long route around the impediment. In my mind, this is a rocky ridge requiring a good many days of work to lead them back to me.

I refuse to dwell on notions of what may have befallen them. There are far too many possibilities and none of them are good.

I choose instead to believe they are merely lost. Their job is to make it back to me, my job is to make certain they can find me.

Yesterday I dragged a long pine pole back to camp but instead of chopping it into burnable lengths, I left it whole. I lashed it snug with rope behind the wagon seat, then tied it to the top of the end rib of the wagon. It stuck straight in the air, another ten feet or so above the rib. Before I lashed it I tethered one of William's long white undershirts to it like a flag, tying each arm to the pole. It did not wag much in the breeze, but by the time I had the entire affair in place and realized I should have used something lighter in weight, it was late in the afternoon.

At least it is something for them to see, I told myself. Tomorrow I will take it down and tie something lighter up there. Perhaps strips ripped from my own underthings. I do not know, but I will figure it out.

That is how I spend much of my time, slowly thinking about each step of a thing that needs doing. It is not a natural way of progressing for me, as I am more of a jump-in-the-water type of person. That brings to mind my dunking in the river days before and I shake my head.

Yes, Papa, you are right. I am as you always say, hasty and rash. But I am trying, Papa. I am trying to be more like you.

Tuesday, October 9, 1849

I have not written in some time, days in fact. If I am honest it has been one week. A whole week, and that makes two weeks and a day since Papa and the boys left that morning to go hunting. I refuse to let myself think of things that might have happened. I refuse to allow my mind to explore those ugly possibilities. Writing that is bad enough.

But what will I do now? I know what I must do, I must survive alone. The way I see my situation, the road has forked before me. That leaves me with two possible paths of travel. One means I stay here waiting for Papa and the boys, who will surprise me one of these days, I know it for a fact. The other is that I must press on without them.

But even if I chose that plan, which I do not like the idea of, I would have to figure out a way to hitch the team, and then drive through the mountains. There is not much of a trail from here, at least not as far as I can see. I am certain Papa knew of a way to get through these mountains from here, but it is a mystery to me. And I do not know what to do.

Saturday, October 13, 1849

Last night the decision I have been struggling with may have been made for me. The wolves came.

Earlier I had cinched the pucker rope tight as I could, then blocked the rear opening with piled crates, the crockery, two sacks of bedding, and clothes. I tried to do the same with the front, but ended up trusting foolishly that a blanket pinned across the opening would be sufficient. But I could not shake the thought: What if something climbed into the wagon during the night?

That is nearly what happened. I was awakened by the sounds of dozens of beasts clawing and fighting and pounding a ring around the wagon. I heard the grass swish against their feet, heard their disjointed panting, yips, and growls, and their gnashing barks all clouding together. Wolves.

I have never been so fearful in all my days. I hope to never be that frightened again. Truly. Then, quick as a finger snap, all those wolves ran away from the wagon. If they hadn't suddenly left, I am not sure I could have stood it another minute.

My relief was short-lived, for what happened next sickened me to my very heart. I heard a loud snort, then a bellowing scream unlike anything I have ever heard. The oxen! The wolves had found them. I heard it all from the wagon. The screams terrified me. Yes, those big oxen scream pitiful death agonies. I pictured those gentle lads, Bib and Bub, for I guessed both were victims, stretched, trembling, big eyes so wide, foam dribbling from their mouths, long tongues stuck out like they do when straining under the great weight of their loads.

And all the while I listened as the awful attackers circled, darting in, laughing in a foul, playful way, as if they were enjoying the affair, until they commenced to squabbling amongst themselves.

I sat up straighter, wriggled free of the blankets and pawed for the shotgun. As my socked hand closed over it, I paused. What was I going to do? What could I really do except kill a wolf or two and maybe shoot the ox in the process? I would surely be surrounded, myself, by the wolves. Or it might be that I could frighten them off. I did not know what to do and for long seconds I panicked, kneeling in the wagon, hanging on the edge of action and cowardice.

In what I am sure was less than a minute, though it felt an eternity, I heard the kicking and flailing of one big beast, then deep, hoarse, ragged breathing. Soon the growls and snaps swarmed over the sounds of a dying ox and that made my horrible decision for me.

It was a black, clouded night, and I sat back once more, knowing my stuttering breath filled the air before my face, though I was unable to see it. I wept as silently as I could for myself, for whichever of the oxen had been so viciously killed— perhaps both of them—and still I was confused.

Would I die here, alone, torn apart by horrible beasts every bit as foul as they appeared in my mind? Or would I be found by Papa and the boys? If not them, perhaps another late-season wagon? Surely this was a common route. We had seen ruts that Papa had assured us were made by others not long before us. Did he know that for a certainty? Oh, Papa, Papa, what have you done? What has happened to us all? Where are you, Papa?

I sat in the wagon with my hands pressed to my ears, hoping the oxen would hook them with their great horns and kill every last one of the slavering wild dogs. But that was not the case.

When I climbed out this morning—poking my head out like a turtle peeking out of its shell—I was surprised at what I saw. Bub was still alive, though not well. He, too, had been savaged, but for some reason was spared death. Though for how long I do not know. I guess the foul beasts will return soon, maybe tonight. Skulking and killing under the cover of darkness, like all with criminal intent in their hearts.

Off to the left I spied the dead thing that had been Bib. I would look him over later, but right then I avoided that chewed mess as much as possible and walked slow-like up to Bub. He was standing head down, nosing now and again at the sparse brown grasses but not interested in eating. It was plain to see why. His hide has been torn along his barrel, and even more so along his flanks, both sides, as if the damnable dogs were trying to eat him from the back to the front. His left-rear leg was injured low, with dried blood along his tendon. I don't think they bit through, but it was not a pretty sight. Still, Bub was able to put some weight on it.

I will relate with whatever amount of good feeling I can muster that it pleased me to see blood along Bub's left horn, streaked and matted with thin, long gray hairs. "You got some licks in, Bub. I am proud of you, big fellow."

I looked all around us but saw no dead wolves. Hopefully the injured will die slow, pained deaths. That is not a charitable thing for me to say, but I do not care. Bub and Bib did not deserve this ill treatment, nature or no.

When Bub saw me approach he lowed, a sad, trembling sound, his eyes wet as if he was crying. I know that sounds foolish, but it is how I took it. In truth, he was likely in terrible pain. I spoke to him in a quiet voice, offered him loving words that didn't make a whit of difference. Maybe the sound of my voice and my hand gently rubbing his neck helped. I was careful to avoid the big red welts raised by wolf claws.

I returned to the wagon and brought back what tinctures from our nostrums box I thought might help ease his pain. But Bub would have none of it. He shuffled away from me, swung his head slowly as if to tell me no, no, please leave me be.

I am persistent, though, and fetched the mucky tub of axle grease. Papa had used the black goop on Floss when her shoulder was opened up two summers back. We think she was spooked in the pasture by something, and in her haste to scamper away she dodged too close to a nub of branch. It was a jagged wound but Papa stitched her up and then smeared axle grease all over that gash.

"Helps the healing process," he'd said. "And keeps the flies from getting in there and laying eggs."

Now I don't think there's much danger of Bub's wounds attracting any flies, but I think the grease might feel soothing. I had never used it on a cut myself, so I can't be certain. I figured I'd try it on one scratch, see how he reacted. I dipped my finger into the thick grease and ladled up a right knob of it big as a crab apple. With my other hand I smoothed his neck, and said, "Whoa, now, Bub. All going to be fine now, this will feel so nice to you, my friend."

He stood still while I touched the glob of grease to the cut. He tensed, his withers shivered, and that was it. I tried again, this time smearing grease onto the wound. He stepped to one side, something I didn't blame him for one bit, but I think it didn't hurt him any. He might even have liked it, it's difficult to tell with an ox. I kept on.

I managed to spread grease on a dozen more cuts before he grew impatient with me and limped off a ways. I left him be, as that's what I'd want. Then I ventured over to take a look at Bib. He was a half-eaten dead ox. There is not much else to say about that. It made me sad to see it, and all the while I'd been huddled in the wagon, knowing it was happening. It was not a quick death for him, and that made me feel even worse.

I headed back to the wagon and dragged out the shotgun and stuffed shells into my coat pockets, two on one side, three on the other. Then I made tea and sat in the sun, so tired all sudden-like. It feels as if each new day carves something off me. How much longer will this happen? Soon there will be little left of me, of the people I hold in my heart, of the animals that have kept me company.

I do not know what to think next, and the minute after that, and the one following that. Will I keep going on like this until . . . ?

There is little value in thinking this way, but I have nothing else left to think about. Tomorrow there will be another sunrise, but today I am sad. Sad because of what I am about to do. Once I make this decision, and do this deed, I will be stranded here, truly alone in the mountains.

Sunday, October 14, 1849

Yesterday I could not write any more. Not until I did what needed doing.

I kept thinking of what Papa would say. Usually I can hear Papa's voice in my head. No, it is even more than that. It is as if he is standing behind me, talking to me over my shoulder. It is such a real feeling that at least once each day since he's been gone I turn quickly expecting to see him. But even before I look, I remember the truth.

And yet I still turn and he is still not there. Will he ever be again? Yes, I tell myself. He and the boys are lost. Just lost, not the other thing.

I can leave this place, and I might, but it will have to be on foot. I cannot pull the wagon with one ox, and an injured one at that. I dare not wait longer to make a decision about Bub. His wounds are not good at all. He is pained and is not spending as much time as he ought looking for grasses to eat. I have tried dabbing the gashes with more axle grease, but there are too many claw marks raked all over him. His blood looks to be going bad, as those wounds are red and puckered. And besides, he will not let me near him anymore. At least not close enough to offer any paltry help I am able. All I can do is talk to him and watch him gaunt up from lack of food and water and too much pain. I must end that misery for him.

The only good to come of it is that he won't have to put up with winter. My decision is a horrible one, but it is necessary.

Papa would have made it, so now it is my turn. I am no longer a child. Once it is done I will decide what to do next, to leave this place or stay.

If I walk out I stand some chance of making it to a settlement. I know not how far Oregon is from here, for the simple fact that I don't know exactly where "here" is. Somewhere in the northern reaches of the Great Rocky Mountain range, that is all I know. I have nearly worn holes in our map with my eyes, so often have I stared at it for a distinguishing mark, something to tell me where I am.

But it is a poor map, and though it is no better than many maps others have used on their way west, most of those people had the advantage of traveling in the company of their fellows. Dwelling on what could have been only angers me, and I have enough to think on, thank you kindly.

Monday, October 15, 1849

A thought came to me earlier this morning, something Papa said a long time back about a milk goat we had. Pesky, her name was. She had somehow hurt a foreleg so that it dangled at the shoulder. Papa had told me he was going to have to kill her, then butcher her for us to eat. I was eight or nine years old at the time and I recall kicking up a fuss that I am sure ol' Widow Needlemeyer heard all the way down the road at her place.

Pesky had been my friend, and when I told Papa that morning she was walking odd, he went right out to the barn and looked at her. I felt sure Papa could make her right as rain again. But it didn't happen that way. And I felt responsible for her death.

Papa explained that a farm animal with a broken leg is useless. That everyone and everything on the farm has to earn their way. He said it was kinder for him to kill her so she wouldn't go on in pain, then she would continue to help us by feeding us. In truth, it took me some time to warm to the idea of eating her, but in such matters Papa brooked little argument. And he was right—Pesky was tasty.

Now, faced with the same task, merciful though it might be to Bub, I found myself wavering, even though he was in obvious pain.

You do what you must in life, Janette.

"Papa?"

I turned, saw nothing but the open brown meadow, and at

the far edge, the wagon with the river beyond. I breathed deeply, my eyes closed, then I marched to the wagon for the shotgun and two shells.

Even from three steps away I could smell the curdled stink rising off Bub's claw wounds. The nasty wolves were succeeding in what they'd set out to do—to kill him.

"Oh, Bub." My tears came readily and I did not care. It seems girls do cry more than boys, and I am no exception, though I sorely wanted to be. That is neither here nor there. I had let Bub suffer for two days, and he was more miserable-looking with each passing hour.

He swung his big head around toward me, his quiet, gentle face tight in pain, his big brown-black eyes wet like river rocks. His big muzzle was warm and his ears were cold, a sure sign he was unwell. Any longer and he'd be laid low with a worse fever.

I gave him a good, long rubbing around the ears, along his broad forehead, the curly tight hair there so thick. I rubbed my palms over his bulged eyes and he leaned into my hand and snorted, his eyes closed.

"I am so sorry for this, Bub." I tried to keep my voice strong but gentle for him, too. I do not care if that doesn't make sense. It does to me. "It is not what I want, nor Papa, of that I am certain." My words made no difference.

I cuffed away light, crusty snow and brittle grasses at my feet, trying to find him a tasty patch. It was all brown. The cold weather had settled in and would not back away again until spring. Bub nosed with little interest the dry, brittle grass.

Poor Bub. I am certain he felt my fear, and knew what was coming to him. I tried to be like Papa and treat it as if killing is part of living, but there was nothing of Papa in me then. It was me, Janette, alone with a scattergun, and facing nothing I could fix a solid thought on.

Quick as I dared, I raised the shotgun to my shoulder, cocked both hammers, and sucked in a breath. The end of the barrel was less than a hand length from Bub's temple, that soft, sunken spot between his eye and his ear. I moved it closer.

Bub started to lift his head toward me. I pulled a trigger and the butt of the stock slammed me to my backside. Bub dropped to his front knees, his head swaying back and forth like someone at a dance who has not been asked to join in.

I had not wanted to look when I did it, but I was mortally afraid I would miss my mark. That would mean having to touch off a second round, and Bub would be in such pain. I hadn't wanted to see any of it, but I did. I saw the far side of his head come away. I saw the eye nearest me grow wide and round. The hole was horrid, the sparse snow a bloodied mess.

He grunted and I held my breath, hoping he wasn't in pain. Before I could empty the second shell into the same spot, Bub made a wheezing, groaning sound, and his head flopped to his right, folding back on itself, as if he were trying to lick at his side. His big body followed it down to the ground.

I sat up and lowered the second hammer gently, then I laid the shotgun on the ground. It was done. I knelt and checked for his heartbeat, but found none. Blood bubbled and welled out the ragged wound in his head, a hole I had put there. I had killed the last living creature, at least within sight, that knew me. My heart thumped in my chest, though not enough to make up for Bub's stilled heartbeat.

The day was young and the sun, for once these past few weeks, was busy curving upward from the east. I had much to do and none of it pleasant. But the work would keep me from feeling worse than I did already.

I snatched up the shotgun, and brought it back to the wagon. I gathered two canvas tarpaulins, Papa's spare skinning knife, and another, larger carving knife. Thus armed I walked back to

Bub and began the time-eating task of butchering a full-grown ox.

We had a decent store of salt, so salting is what I intended to do with the meat. Smoking it was not possible, as it is a slow task, days and days of effort, and I do not have the time or patience for it, let alone the knowledge.

I was hungry, even as I sliced into Bub's flank and peeled away the hide. My gut growled like how I imagine a baby bear might sound come spring.

I had intended to save as much of the hide in one piece as I was able, but I do not know enough about curing to make it a useful thing. Would it attract creatures I do not need near me? It was bad enough that Bub's blood splashed all over the ground. I would have to bathe myself and my clothes in the river, and that would require a full blazing fire to dry everything. But not until I was done with this job.

The air carried a chill to it, the same sort of bone-creeper Papa always says means a storm is on its way.

My meat cuts are not pretty, but I did my best to make them ample, to not waste any of that good beast's ended life. I laid them on a tarpaulin, stacking them according to thickness and size. I made none of them very thick at all, for they all had to be salted. I was thankful it was far too late in the season for great swarms of flies. Nothing will come around to fresh blood faster than flies.

The ones that like the meat more than hungry wolves are blowflies. Nasty things. Circling and buzzing and not at all fast, sort of heavy and sluggish, and will as likely land on your arm as on your butcher knife—anything at all as long as there is blood on it. Oh, but they are nasty things. Even as I write this I can feel them walking around in the sticky, steaming blood on my arm hairs. They weren't really there, of course, but that doesn't mean I don't know what they feel like. I helped Papa with butchering a number of times on the farm, wild critters and animals we raised for their meat. It is never a task that grows easier with time.

Makes me want to wash and wash and wash. But Bub's carcass came first. It was gruesome work, I can tell you, and I did not salvage various parts that Papa does, such as the head, the eyes, the brain, all that to boil up and make blood pudding. I could not bring myself to do that to Bub's face. I console myself with the thought that I had ended his suffering, however slight it was compared with Bib's, in a kinder way than being dragged down and chewed to death by wolves.

I was tempted to slice out his tongue, for that is a savory cut of meat. But that would have meant grappling with Bub's head, and I could not bear to look into those filmy eyes and pillage any more than I had to.

I tied on one of my older aprons up high above my breasts, under my armpits, and used that as a smock. It was soon brown with smeared blood. I also tried not to kneel down while I worked meat from the bone, but an ox is a big beast and I am not particularly large, though Papa says I am of a good height.

In my uncharitable moments, I worry he is judging if I will be able to marry one day. Not that it ever did, but the notion of marriage hasn't much crossed my mind lately. I do not wonder why.

But back to Bub, I did my very best to keep the skinning knife's edge honed. The day was turning off clear but cold, carrying a tang of coming snow, I was sure of it. It made me work all the faster.

Lastly I honed the limbing axe and set to work hacking through Bub's leg bones. I wish I had the ability to make shorter lengths, but at least I could have marrow bones. They are delectable and though splitting them lengthwise is possible with the axe, it would be tricky, too. I reckoned I would be able to jam a thin branch down the heated length of bone and pull out the tasty cooked marrow. That alone could sustain me for a month of Sundays.

I stood back and regarded what I had done. Despite the cold, sweat dripped down my forehead and stung my eyes. I wiped with the back of my arm, but only ended up smearing more blood on my face.

I had stacked a sizable amount of meat and would now have to drag it across the meadow to the wagon. I had intentionally led Bub out across the valley floor, away from the wagon in hopes that when the wolves came for his carcass they would keep well clear of me.

I left off the meat cutting then for a few minutes, glad to be away from the warm, close stink of it. Nothing smells so wrong as blood. I can't explain it any better than that. Of all the bad things I have smelled in my life, dung, bad breath, long-dead critters, stale sweated-up clothes of boys, nothing is quite so out of place and ill-fitting as the smell of blood. It feels as if it will never leave your nose, as if it will always be packed up inside there, seeped permanently into your skin and hair and lungs.

I walked back to the wagon. I had an idea, you see, and wiped clean the blade of the knife on my apron as I walked, breathing deep of the clean air. The sky was high and blue and spread out everywhere. I daren't look down, as I half expected the blue to continue right around me, as if I was in a glass dish. I rummaged in the wagon, making a mess of things that I had tried to keep tidy. From the start of the journey, I learned neatness was near impossible in such a small space.

At least without the boys slamming and dragging their way through it these past couple of weeks I have been able to keep it somewhat orderly. Now my main concern was in keeping the bloody apron from dragging over the hanging clothes, trunks, crates, and buckets.

I found what I was after, much of a five-pound sack of coarse salt, and dragged it out. I looked for more, but found none. The sack would have to do. I scooped out a small handful and tipped that into an empty glass jar for the time being. I would save that for seasoning, unless I needed it, too, for the meat.

The rest I set on the open tailgate of the wagon, then commenced to empty foodstuffs and kitchen items from one container into others, jamming them together where I could. I needed vessels to pack full of meat. I glanced out the back of the wagon at the tarpaulin, stacked sloppily with raw meat. There was a whole lot of it, and none of it looked appetizing. Once I rubbed it with salt, it would look strange and taste even worse than that. But at least it should preserve the meat—and hopefully cover up the smell enough that I could tuck it safely away.

But where? That's a thought I had been avoiding for some time. Even though I was butchering the last of the two oxen, I still had in mind that all would turn out well somehow, as long as the weather held. Might be I would not need any shelter beyond the wagon. So far we'd only received dustings of snow, nothing that I could not trudge through on my way up and out of the mountains.

But what would I do with all this meat? What was it I was really doing? I did not want to admit what I knew had to be done. I have to leave or stay, no other choices. I do not want to leave because I am afraid of what I do not know beyond this little mountain valley. And I believe I am using Papa and the boys and their return to me as an excuse to wait and not make the hard decision.

For the time being, I shirked that decision once more. I did the thing I have become accustomed to, the thing that makes bearing all this so much easier—I concentrated on the task right before my nose and did not look much beyond that.

I lugged the vessels, all I could find, boxes and nail kegs, mostly, six in all, to the back of the wagon. I hopped down with a grunt, dipped the ladle into the water keg, only to find the top crusted with ice. I jammed it in there a few times and the ice broke up. The water, cold enough to freeze my lips, felt good, but soon hurt my teeth as I gulped it. Butchering is thirsty work.

I looked to the sky again, pausing between gulps to let my teeth warm up. The sun had already begun to head toward the mountains to the west. I had but a couple of hours at best before nightfall came. And with all that raw meat sitting out there pretty as you please, and a cut-up carcass laid out for the world to see, wolves included, I knew I had to get busy. Suddenly that dead ox (I can't think of it as Bub anymore) did not look far enough at all from the wagon.

I walked back to the sloppy meat pile. It was sizable. I decided then and there I'd better deal with that much and leave off carving on the rest until tomorrow. Unless the wolves got to it first, then I would have to be satisfied with what I had before me.

"All depends on how fast you eat it, girl," I told myself, standing there and looking down at it.

I had intended to drag the canvas across the meadow to the wagon, but I got worried about leaving a big ol' smear of a blood trail for the critters to follow directly to the wagon and me, inside and sleeping. So I walked back to the wagon, grabbed a keg I thought I could about lug if it was full, and I went back to that meat pile and filled it up.

I may have overestimated my strength. I bent to heft that keg full of meat and about broke my back. But I did get it raised, after I took a few hunks off, flopped them back on the stack. I was near to tears when I realized how much work I still had ahead of me. I should have started earlier in the day.

I made it back to the wagon with my keg of meat, and as quick as I could, given that I was panting to beat the band, I drizzled a goodly portion of salt in the bottom of another keg, then rubbed and smacked and smeared salt all over each hunk of meat as I pulled it out of the bloody keg. Every vein and joint as well as the entire surface of every piece had to have a goodly glaze on it, I knew that much from helping Papa salt meat for keeping.

Even though it stung in the cracks of my sore hands, the salting went along faster than I expected. Heartened by that I returned with renewed vigor to the piled meat across the meadow. Soon I had salted and stored about two-thirds of the pile. I was growing tired and quick. I was a wound clock nearing the end of my day.

As I finished off a load, layering it atop other salty hunks in a crate I'd lined with thin cotton cloth, I realized I was squinting. "Oh no!" I shouted. I looked to the sky behind me as I said it and saw the sun beginning its dip down low. I still had so much meat to retrieve.

"Nothing for it," I said, hustling back across the meadow. I carried the last two vessels with me, a keg, on the small side, and a canvas satchel with leather strap handles. I hated to fill that last with meat because I rather liked it for ease of toting most anything, but I was plumb out of things to store meat in.

I had almost filled the keg when I looked up again. I am not sure what I expected to see. It's not as if the sun was about to slow itself for me. But then I am an optimistic sort. I noticed the sky to the west had laid itself out long and low, coloring my blood-dried hands a pretty orange, reminding me for a moment of the lilies that grew by the front door of our old farmhouse. Only it wasn't our home anymore. It belonged to Cousin Merdin and his bitter stick of a wife, Ethel, and those two bratty twins. I don't mind saying it as there is little danger of them ever seeing this diary.

A sudden sharp yip stiffened me in and out. I stood up straight and looked to the northwest, from where it had come. Another sharp yip peeled off not far from it—though still far enough. Coyotes? Wolves? I didn't know enough about them yet to tell from that distance. I hope I never get a close-up lesson. The night they'd killed Bib was near enough.

How could I expect them to stay away when I'd spent the day making a bloody pile of meat and bones? It must have been like fresh-baked apple pie smells to Thomas and William and Papa after a day in the south field.

I am convinced no one ever carried a keg of meat so fast as I did that late afternoon. I glanced at the sky as I waddled back to the wagon. My breath came out and in, short and fast, timed somehow with my stumbling steps. By my reckoning I had less than an hour before pitch-black night came. That didn't leave me enough time to do the things I needed to do. I had to get the last of that meat to the wagon. One more lugged load, and I had intended to strip down and wash the blood off me.

I set to the tasks as fast as I could, the cold coming in with a vengeance, the dark closing in on its heels. As soon as I stepped off the canvas I'd stacked all the meat on I realized I might need it. But if I left the bloody thing stretched on the crusty grass and snow for the night, the wolves or coyotes or whatever hairy, fanged thing was out there might well treat it like jerky, and then I'd have nothing.

I chewed that over in my mind as I hurried back to the wagon with that last satchel of meat. I'd salt that and the last keg full later. For the time being I sprinkled what was left of the salt over the top, shook it to distribute it, plunked a frying pan on top of the keg, and laid a stack of blankets over the satchel. The meat beneath was salted and half frozen anyway.

I ran back to the carcass of old Bub, gave him a quick prayer of thanks and a head nod, then folded that tarp, half to half to half until it was a square I could carry. It was mighty stiff from the cold by that time, but I could still smell it, bloody and raw, like when you lick metal. As I say, blood is a taste you can't shake.

I had an idea I still had light enough to take that canvas tarpaulin and my own bloody self down to the river. It was open down the bank from the wagon, flowing like a burst sore in a circle out from under thin, ragged-edge ice.

"This could well be another of my foolhardy moments, Papa," I told myself. But there was nothing for it. I had to get as much of the blood stink off and away from me as I could before lashing myself into the wagon for the night.

On my way past the wagon I grabbed a hank of stout hemp rope Papa had hanging on a hook on the side of the wagon, one of a half dozen of them of varying lengths and thicknesses. He is a man who likes to have a good hank of rope on hand. Says you can do pretty much whatever you need to with a good axe, a set of willing arms and legs, and a length of stout rope.

I hoped he was right. I also scrabbled around behind the driver's bench, and laid a hand on a stiff-bristle brush normally used for cleaning burs out of the oxen's tails, among other tasks. Then I headed to the river.

It took more time than I would have liked to strip off my bloody clothes. They were frozen and sopping tight to me, all at once. Next to falling in the rushing froze-over river, standing all but naked beside it in a breeze that felt like tiny blades slicing through the air, is a painful experience, I tell you. And then it got worse. I could see enough yet to tell that my scrubbing with a wad of clean cloth dipped in the frigid water wasn't rubbing off all the blood. Something had to be done, and I knew what it was.

I commenced to scrubbing with the brush, and darn if that

didn't tickle. And by tickle I mean hurt bad. It felt as if I were peeling off at least the top three layers of my skin. But I also saw that the brush, painful as it was, was effective at stripping off the blood. I was still afraid once I got the little wagon stove heated up, all that blood on me and my clothes would commence to stink. I was determined to get it off me at all costs. No way under heaven was I going to make myself a temptation to wolves.

The blood had leeched through my apron and dresses and longhandles and undershirt to my midsection, and that's where a body has some tender skin. Rasping and dragging that brush on my belly made me howl almost as much as the cold air did. But I believe I did a fair job of cleaning up, I know I felt numb as a hammer-struck thumb when I was done. And I could only imagine what it was going to feel like the next day.

Next I dunked my clothes a number of times, working them together hard, sort of mashing them and wringing them all at once, then balled them up in the center of that tarpaulin. I cinched it tight, and shinnied a few feet onto what was left of an old tree that leaned out over the water. My longhandles did very little in protecting my legs, and I figured I'd been so tore up by the brushing I'd given myself that my bare torso couldn't face any worse. But I was wrong—that bark was rough.

Judging from the gashed surface on the underside, it felt like that tree had seen plenty of ice in its time. It wasn't a big tree but it was sufficient enough, I hoped, for my needs. I lashed that rope around the trunk so the knob of bloody canvas and clothes hung out over the river. A wolf would have to be mighty determined to get at that.

Pleased with my efforts, I struggled up the bank to the wagon. I had momentarily forgotten I was all but naked, when the wind kicked up. It felt like bee stings all over me. With each passing step I got the creeping feeling we were in for snow this very night. I climbed inside the wagon, and managed to light a candle with a sulfur match. It was a lazy girl's indulgence, I admit.

I do not like using them because, as Papa says, once a thing is used up out here on the trail, there is not another anywhere nearby to replace it. It's not as though I am encamped close by a trading post, let alone a mercantile.

But I was desperate and near to freezing. And though I was tempted to huddle in the wagon under quilts and cup myself around that tiny candle flame, I know foolish when I sniff it, and I was full of it. I commenced to do the next smartest thing I could. I built a fire in the stove and used the candle flame to set a twist of curly bark and dry moss to flame.

I transferred that to the firebox of the stove and as I always did when I lit a fire, I prayed and held my breath. Fire can be such a life-saving thing and it can also be a tender thing easy to kill with a sneeze or a cough or a laugh. I don't like to risk any of them when I start a fire, so I hold my breath. And I don't much care who mocks me for it.

It took the little stove a few long minutes to settle into its task, but once it did, it didn't let me down that night. And for that I was grateful. Only then did I shed the quilts and dive for fresh clothes. I didn't bother looking at myself. I fear the bristle brush may have been overdoing the cleaning of the blood, but I was running out of daylight. I suspect I will heal.

As soon as I got fresh shirts and woolens and finally the coat back on, I also pulled on two pairs of socks over my hands. As mittens they are warm, but awkward to use for more than swinging your arms to keep from freezing up.

The most important task I had was to finish pulling in the kegs and boxes and one satchel full of salted meat. I did pay attention to them to see if they were dripping from the day's events. But they were too frozen to worry about. I dragged the others on in and commenced to close up the ends of wagon, cinching them as tight as possible. Behind these I hung extra blankets and stacked anything I could up in front of them.

I checked that I had the shotgun and an axe and two knives—a big old hip knife and the skinning knife—close at hand. Then I worried about keeping warm for the night. You don't have any idea how cold a wagon is until you've slept sitting upright in one for a couple of weeks. My word, even though I had a nice spot arranged for myself, I won't lie, I was some cold. Right down to my boots and then some. Cold, cold, and more cold. I about wrapped myself around that little stove.

To make matters worse, that storm I could smell coming? It did. I heard a scratching sound against the wagon cover. I'd dozed off and it jerked me right awake. I thought for certain I was a goner, that something was sniffing me and the meat and whatever else it wanted in the wagon.

I came more awake and heard it for what it was—snow pelting the tarp. I knew it couldn't be rain because it was too blamed cold. There wasn't a thing I could do that night except pray I had jammed enough wood inside the already tight wagon that morning.

In my mind I went over the campsite wondering if I'd left anything of consequence out there. I came across a few items I wished I'd gotten under cover: The two Dutch ovens were still out and should have been hung back under the wagon by their bails. And I know I left Papa's double-bit axe leaning against a wheel. A little snow would hardly hurt it.

I sniffed at the stack of salted meat vessels. I thought maybe I could smell meat, but I can't be sure. My nose still is still clouded by that warm blood smell I mentioned earlier. Maybe the cold would disguise them. I covered them with what clothes I could afford to give up that weren't wrapped around me.

My belly began to growl louder than any sound a wolf could cough up, I'll wager. I let it go for a time, but I couldn't quiet it. So I uncovered a pan of biscuits I'd saved from two days before. I have been trying to ration my food, make it last as long as possible. But with all the work that day, I reckoned I deserved, as Papa says, to tie on the feed bag. I ate every biscuit in the pan and they weren't enough, but they went a long way to quieting that angry bear in my gut.

I made a cup of tea, since water is about all I want to cook on the little stove when I have the wagon sealed up. Smoke and food smells cloud up near the ceiling, and I didn't dare risk it. The stove pipe is stuck through a steel ring up high in the wagon cover, but it is a loose fit and gusts of wind rattle in around the pipe, and snow sifts in now and again. The little flakes hit the stove and sizzle.

I have had snow off and on since Papa and the boys left that morning, but I knew they were passing storms, dustings that crust up then melt off later in the day. For some reason I know this storm is different, one to be paid attention to. I don't like to admit it, but it makes me angry that the decision I hadn't wanted to make has been made for me.

I expect I am losing my chance to leave the valley on foot. The more snow that falls, the more difficult it will be to get anywhere of consequence on foot. Papa talked of making us snowshoes as something to have in case we ran into what he called "squalls" in the mountains. But he never got around to making them, and I have no idea how to go about such a thing. They will only be useful if I intend to walk out.

If I do that it would mean leaving them behind. What if Papa and the boys come back to find the camp buried in snow and me gone? I could leave markers pointing in the direction I take. But I know Papa pretty well and I bet he'd not rest until he caught up with me. He would be disappointed in me, I think.

Or maybe I am lying to myself because I am afraid. I don't like to admit being afraid, and in truth I have not been much afraid of anything in my fourteen years. But I have experienced more fear in the past three, nearly four months since we left home than I did in my entire life leading up to the day we left.

Most of that fear has fallen like a mountain of mud on my head since Papa and the boys left me. I don't like to go on and on about such things because it worries me that I will become one of those people you hear about who lives alone and worries and fears over every little thing that might happen to them. In truth little of it ever happens to them. They never get to see or hear or feel anything wonderful outside their shuttered windows. I could go on like this, and I don't care what people think. It makes me feel better.

I am falling asleep with that thought in my mind and I am worried very little of wolves or bears or lions or anything else that might pull me from this little nest I have made in the wagon.

"Good night, Janette."

"Good night."

TUESDAY, OCTOBER 16, 1849

This morning I woke in the dark, as I always do. With all the family gear piled tight, there isn't room enough for stretching out, so I sleep sitting up. It isn't the most comfortable way to rest yourself, but if you are tired enough it will do the trick. When you wake up you find yourself a mite "crampy," as Papa says of a morning.

My, but that man can carry on, especially if he has an audience. He'll groan and stumble around holding his back and his knees and stretching his shoulders "to work out the kinks." Then he'll look over sort of sideways at me or the boys and wink. I do quote Papa quite a bit. I guess that's only natural given that I have pretty much seen him every day of my life, except for a few times when he was off to another town buying stock or selling crops. But that was a rare event and sometimes only took one day. These recent weeks have been the longest I have gone without seeing anyone else of my family.

This morning I was so stiff I didn't think I'd ever unbend myself without cracking apart in a dozen pieces. And that wasn't the worst part. When I finally shifted around, I throbbed and ached all over, and I knew right off what afflicted me. I was in mortal agony because of that scrubbing I'd given myself with that stiff-bristle brush.

Looking back on my frantic rushing around of last night, I was right to be hurried and worried, especially once the critters began that far-off howling. But I should have slowed down and grabbed soap and a rough cloth instead of that brush. I tenderly felt my arms, my belly. Though I would have bet good money my fingers were touching raw wounds, I knew they were welted drag marks from the brush. I'd have to get it over with at some point, so I did my best to stand up quick.

It smarted enough for me to gasp, but then it got better, sort of settled into a feeling halfway between a burn and the sting left over after you've been slapped, only this smacking covered my entire body.

I figure if a thing doesn't kill me, I must get over it. Gnawing at it like a hound worrying a bone does no good. It was obvious that rough scraping I gave myself, while painful, was far from the end of me, so I did my best to ignore it. Soon enough my mind settled on the fact that it was downright cold and still. My breath hung in a thin cloud all about me. I held it in for a moment and listened—last night's hellacious wind had traveled elsewhere. I knew what I would see when I parted the flaps of the wagon's cover and looked out across the little mountain meadow—nothing but white.

I imagined I would see entire cities spread before me, sparkling rooftops and spires of cathedrals, onion domes and turrets, all dusted by nature's magic. It would seem as if I were somehow on a tall mountain peak and they were far below, stretching away as far as I could see into the distance. And they would not be white like snow, but kissed with color, faint, like the blue of river ice near the end of winter. But not only blue, I imagined gold and pink and green and all those colors between that only fancy artists have names for.

Such foolish, fanciful thoughts kept me warm the whole while I took lighting the stove. I had a sizable enough stack of snapped branches to warm up the inside of the wagon, but I'd have to get out quick and rummage in the woodpile. I was thankful I'd spent time stockpiling firewood.

I had little choice. If I didn't keep warm I might as well lie right down in the snow next to the carcasses of old Bub and Bib and let the critters have at me. Besides, fetching firewood gave me relief from not spending every minute of my day thinking about Papa and the boys. And wood gathering keeps me warm while I am at it. Papa always says wood warms you three times: once when you chop it, again when you stack it, then lastly when you burn it. I agree with that.

By the time I was ready to peek at what Mother Nature left me, the two cups of tea I'd had were reason enough to get out of doors and relieve myself. Not a simple task when you have trousers and longhandles on beneath layers of skirts. But I dare not complain. Papa and the boys were no doubt struggling mighty to keep warm, too, wearing only what they brought with them. I wear as much clothing as I can stand to have on and still go about my chores.

The snow was pretty, as I knew it would be. No great magical cities poked out of it, but it was as fine a sight as the first big snow of the season should be. The sun was up, the sky beyond blue to nearly silver, and I watched my breath float out of my mouth and swirl off and disappear. And there still was no sound. I almost hated to make a noise.

About then nature's call took over and I figured it would be more embarrassing to wet myself than to crack open the silence. Colder, too. I jumped down and kicked my way through a whole lot of loose, gritty snow that came nearly to my knees. That was plenty for one storm. I wondered if the winters here in the mountains were full of such weather. What if that much snow came down every few days? Something to think about.

Tuesday, October 16, 1849

Later this morning, after I cleaned off my woodpile—like a fool I had neglected to cover it with the other canvas tarpaulin the day before—I did my best to shovel the snow away from the campsite. Papa's grain shovel is cumbersome, wide and heavy, but it is what I have. I have come to the conclusion that shoveling is a whole lot like gathering wood. It warms a body and gives the mind time to think.

All the while I worked at setting the campsite to rights, I did my best to think about anything but whether I was going to wait for Papa and the boys in the valley or set out on my own, on foot, through the pass I believe Papa was headed for when we stopped.

Now, I am not normally one to shirk a task, but this decision is difficult to grapple with. I noticed the snow grew heavier as the day aged. And I was sweating more. I stood up straight and stretched my back and squinted around me. The sun had burned through whatever clouds were left over from the storm. And then I realized what was happening. The day was turning off warm. Mighty warm.

The low spots in the meadow still showed slumped snow, but even there I saw stubbly brown bristle grass poking up like a porcupine's coat. Might be this snow wouldn't be with me all that long. I was pleased. But then a new thought came tripping over that one. The autumn was still a new thing, it being only October. What would happen when the days grew colder?

I climbed back into the wagon, closed the flaps behind me, and made tea. Then, when I had a cup warming my hands, I sat down where I'd been sleeping and resolved to make my decision. And what I decided was that I was familiar with the little valley, and I was sure that Papa and the boys would be along before too many more days passed.

Suddenly it was that simple. I have decided I need to stay here and wait for my family. I believe it will not take them much longer to come back to me.

WEDNESDAY, OCTOBER 17, 1849

That first big snowstorm was a warning. That's how I took it, anyway. And once my decision was made to stay put, a desperate fever gripped me like no other. The wagon was colder than anything I could imagine at that point. In fact, I could not even imagine spending another night in it, though I knew I had to.

If I am going to be stuck here for a lengthy spell, I have to build a suitable shelter. Something that can protect me from the weather, yet small enough that I can heat it well. On the trail Papa told me of soddies, houses built of dirt. Thomas said that was crazy, nobody lived in dirt, but Papa laughed, then told us all about how people had been living in dirt forever, somewhere on earth. He even said that bricks were nothing more than hard dirt. Now that I think on it, I suppose wood was nothing more than dirt way back when the tree was growing.

But one thing Papa said about dirt stuck in my mind. A dirt house could be warm in the winter and cool in the hot months. Right then I could not imagine there would ever be anything like a July or August ever again, so cold was I in that wagon. But I liked the other part of that notion—warm in the winter.

So I have set out to dig a dirt house, or as near as I can. But where to do it? I jumped back down out of the wagon and closed the flap behind me. Keep that little warmth in there. No sense sharing it with the out of doors. Not like Mother Nature was interested in being warm this time of year anyway.

I stood with my hands on my hips, looking at the wagon, and

decided I might be able to use some of it, maybe for a frame. But I'd have to take it apart, which might be difficult, even if I did have two axes. I put my hand to my eyes, in part to cut the snow glare. I walked toward the river and spied what I did not know I'd been looking for. Below where I stood, yet above the river, there is a scooped-out bowl in the meadow.

I tested the edge with my boot, but I did not take into account that the snow might be hiding the true edge. My foot slipped, went out straight as if I was kicking it up at a dance, and I did not land on my backside until I was halfway down the slope. It didn't much hurt, but I flailed trying to right myself and ended up wet on my rear end and up my legs. I sighed, stood up, and I'll be jiggered if my feet didn't slip right out from under me once more.

That time, I sat right there in slushy snow, the sun warming everything around me, and I laughed. It was the first time in a long, long time I did. Even when I thought of Papa and the boys, I still kept laughing. They'd be laughing at me, I am sure of it. And I wager Thomas would be lobbing snowballs at me the entire time.

After a minute more, I stood again, my feet spread, and managed to stay upright. Yes, I thought, I could see how this spot might be what I need. That slope I'd come down was more gradual behind me to the east, and might make an easier spot to climb. But how does a body use dirt to make a shelter?

WEDNESDAY, OCTOBER 17, 1849

It is later the same day, and it is still a complicated question: How to use dirt to do my bidding? Critters don't have such worries. I swear, I wish I could curl up in a ball and sleep away the winter like a mouse in a nest.

And that's when it came to me: I need a nest. I was thinking about it all wrong. If I can't burrow into the earth, which sounded to me like a whole lot of work, I could at least use part of the hollow to build against. It looked dry enough, and with any luck the wind might pass over me, though it could as easily pack tight with drifted snow.

It took me the better part of an hour to decide what I was going to build, but once I set my mind to something, there is precious little that will change it. I circled around and walked pretty easily up the slight slope at the east edge of the depression.

I had plenty of daylight left to me, so I trudged back to the wagon and honed a decent edge on the axe. I was about to depart for the nearby copse when I stopped and took stock of my situation. It is a habit I am getting into, though it takes more reminding than I would like.

I strapped the skinning knife around my waist with Papa's spare belt. I debated about bringing the shotgun and finally decided I had better. I stuffed two shells into my coat pocket, tugged woolly socks on my hands, and hefted the gun in one hand and the axe in the other. It was a balance I've become used to. The stand of pines I intended to ransack isn't too far, south of me at the meadow's edge. The land there bends in all manner of directions at once, like a blanket on a bed when you first wake.

There were a number of straight and tall, but nearly dead pines I had not yet taken for firewood. I estimated I'd need at least two dozen of them, each a good twenty feet long, to build what I have in mind.

I set to work and managed to fell six and started in on a seventh when I took stock of the wind. It had picked up, though it didn't smell anything like yesterday's wind, no snow on the wing, as Papa would say. But then I am hardly an expert. Now Papa, he can tell what's coming . . . at least regarding the weather.

The wind chilled me for a moment, enough of an odd feeling that I looked to my left, westward, and I leaned the axe against the tree it was chewing into. There was a big ol' rabbit, setting up on his haunches and staring me down. I had eaten plenty of such critters in my time, prepared a mess of them, and knew how good they could taste. I reached for the shotgun with the other hand. I didn't feel it so I cut my eyes from where I'd been staring for a sliver of a second. By the time I looked back, that rabbit was gone, like steam off a bowl of soup.

I sighed and set the gun down. Then it came to me I wouldn't have had rabbit for supper anyhow, as I hadn't loaded the shells into the gun. Fat lot of good the big thing would do me if I was attacked by a wolf. I made up for my poor judgment and thumbed in two shells. Then I set to work on that seventh tree. Once I had it felled, I looked at the half-skinned, dried trees and realized there was no way I could haul one of them plus the axe and the gun all at once. Something would have to go.

I decided finally that though I might not have any choice about living in fear, I could make up my mind to work with two hands, and that meant leaving the axe and shotgun at the wagon so I could get on with what needed doing.

I'd have the knife by my side, anyway. I strapped on the second long knife, to be sure. The pair of them wouldn't hinder me much and I might be able to use one to skin off small branches and irksome knots.

By the time I lugged the axe and shotgun back to camp and returned to my felled trees, the sky to the east was darkening and the sun to the west was starting its daily show of pretty, as I call it. The sun is saying, "Look at me, how could you ignore me all day long!" And it works, for I always take time to look at the sun as it sets.

I tucked into my task with a vengeance and found my thoughts turning to food. That ox meat would keep me for a while, and we have a goodly store of ground cornmeal and flour, as well as a few sacks and tins of dried fruits, sugar, coffee, tea, seasonings, and the like, but how long would they last me?

I had to eat well enough to keep up my strength to gather wood, to survive the cold. But for how long? Surely Papa and the boys would be back soon. Perhaps they made it to a settlement.

That sort of thinking tends to occupy my mind more than it ought, but it is a daily struggle to get on with the things that need tending. Let alone the things in my mind that demand attention. Attention I can ill afford right about now.

Didn't I say a mind could wander? I was lugging logs back to camp, more to the point I was dragging them, when I began thinking of food, probably because I was hungry and weak from being hungry and weak. It never ends. Then I started in on that endless thought trail about Papa and the boys and here I am again. I swear . . .

I'd fetched all but the last tree back to camp when I decided to call it a day. I was shaking and needed to sit down. I had no food prepared, not even biscuits, and thanks to Thomas I had no jerky to soften in hot water. I didn't much fancy eating flour, and dried fruit didn't hold much appeal at that moment. It was best after a meal, as a special treat.

But that didn't stop me from eating two dried slices of apple, which I followed with water aplenty, and that about filled me up. The one good thing about ample snowfall is the guarantee of water. As if the river didn't provide that cold comfort on its own.

I still had a few minutes of light left to me, and the wind dwindled. I hated to say it, but the temperature was almost warm again. I considered building a fire outdoors, but then I thought about how much effort it takes to gather the firewood and decided I should save it for the little stove, which takes far less wood and heats me better all around. Which isn't saying much.

But I did walk over to where I'd decided to build and one word rolled through my mind like fog over a farm pond in early morning: Nest. Nest. Nest. Yes, I will build a nest. But instead of backing it up to the sloped earth as I thought I might, I decided to move it out away from there a few feet. I had sudden visions of wolves stepping right off that meadow top and right onto my roof once the snow built up enough. But I needed protection from the wind I'd seen whipping in, mostly from the northeast.

I went back to the wagon and shut myself in for the night. I did not fall asleep right away. Instead I sat bundled in quilts, thinking of how I would build my nest. It is almost exciting, if I don't let myself think about why I have to do such a thing. I rearranged a few items to stretch my legs to sleep, and was doing so, and feeling dozy and wondering how to make the walls of my nest thick and warm and tight, when I heard them. The wolves.

Their panting voices came from nowhere and everywhere all at once. Like the last time, they swarmed the wagon, snuffling and sniffing and sounding like they were inches from me, which they were, but I don't like to think about that. And then they were gone, or some of them, anyway. As they ran off they squabbled and I pictured them biting at each other in some sort of frenzy.

They didn't go far, though. They found the carcass of Bub and commenced to stripping it of anything I might have been able to go back for.

It was a good thing I went there earlier in the day and cut what else I could from him. It was almost easier with him mostly frozen. I hope they broke their foul fangs on Bub or Bib's bones. And as much as I hate to say it, I prayed for snow. For if the last night's storm was any sort of truth, then it is storms that keep them away. But that is a fool's wish. They will be back. Again and again. I know it.

Sunday, October 21, 1849

I admit the nest I pictured in my mind is far prettier than the one I have been slowly building over these past days. I have always had high expectations of myself in life. Papa says I get that from Mama, but I know he can be most picky about a task. However, this shelter, nest, or whatever I dare call it—anything but home, for I swear I will not be here long enough to make it thus—is far removed from my mind's first vision.

I spent much of one day digging holes to set the butt ends of logs in, only to find that I had been far too ambitious in my thinking. At that rate, the size of the structure would be as long as the wagon and twice as wide. I do not have the ability to chop down that many trees for the shelter alone. I will need my strength and I will need the trees for firewood. So I changed my plans and in so doing had to yank ten poles out and dig new holes for them, not so far apart this time. I am lucky, I suppose, that I did not realize my mistake days later than I did. That will teach me to be so full of myself.

But this thing I am building is not pretty. I tell myself it doesn't have to be, but I hoped it would have turned out more handsome. Here is what it looks like: Roughly half again as long as I am tall, the same in the other direction, but that does not mean it is square. I meant it to be, of course, but it came out with no regular shape at all.

Little matter, for now that it is well on its way, and I know there is no turning back, I am pleased. I angled the poles inward with their butt ends planted in holes all less than a foot deep. They leaned every which way, but I packed as much sod around them as I was able.

I am thankful that the earth hereabouts is wet through but not yet frozen. It has made for a decent building material and I fancy I have become quite good at cutting sizable clods that mostly hold together and stack well. I devised a method of mounding them up between the poles so they don't fall over until I have them all stuck in the ground and secured at the top.

A goodly supply of rope would be more than I could wish for. Of course, if I am wishing, I'd want to be elsewhere and surrounded by my family.

I hesitate to use much of my rope for I feel it will be useful in other ways that have yet to reveal themselves. For now, I lop green whips, branches and spry saplings, and bend them in a weave to help bind the poles and crosspieces in place. Most of them split, but still manage to hold together. I stagger the snapped bits and in the end fancy I will have something that is functional.

It is resembling a square-shaped woven beehive, though not so pretty as any I have seen. It also lacks much in the way of a roof. I angled the poles in enough that it won't require many crosspieces at the top for the roof. And though I say top, really it's not much taller than Papa. Inside I fear it will be like a dark cave, but I daren't make space for windows. My biggest concern, really more of a fear, is that I won't make this stout enough to keep marauding animals away. But all my dirt digging has given me an idea.

TUESDAY, OCTOBER 23, 1849

The idea I mentioned yesterday might work. It had better, at any rate, as I spent all of this day devoted to it. I reached the point of no return today. I stripped the canvas cover off the wagon. I have not seen our wagon thus since the week we started west.

Papa had finished outfitting the wagon with the various built-in cupboards and hooks, inside and out, and the cover, a used one he bought from someone who knew someone who had decided not to go on their own journey, had proven too short all the way around. He debated for a time whether to cut the ribs down, but decided that since he and the boys are tall and I am not terribly short for a girl, we might as well have the extra eight or so inches of height.

So what did he do? Without even asking if I might be up to the task, he hired Martha McGovern to sew extra canvas around the base. I could have done it, but admittedly she did a decent job of it, maybe better than I would have. Before I declare her work too wonderful, I will see how it holds up over time.

Martha is an interesting creature, and if Papa was not my Papa I might be more inclined to like her. Though she is clearly younger than Papa (and older than me), I believe she set her cap on Papa and would have done about anything he asked of her. I bet she wanted him to ask her to come along on the trip. I know she made all manner of twittery remarks about it. And now that I think on it, if she had—which means Papa would have married her—she might well be here with me now. For good or ill, I know not which. That is a trail I do not want my mind to wander down.

At any rate, Papa and I measured and measured for hours to make sure he bought the correct amount of extra canvas. "There is no going back once this cover is in the works," he'd said, winking.

I think Papa was at his happiest since Mama died when he was planning the journey, readying everything we might need. And now that I think back on it, I do wonder if he was even aware of Martha McGovern's affections for him? Now I feel cruel and small in my remarks. But what's done is done.

I dragged the cover down the slope to the nest. It took much doing to arrange it atop my frame and then it did not sit right. No matter how I rearranged it, the thing fought me like an ornery child. Of course it did not help that it was meant for something that resembled a loaf of tall-risen bread and my nest is anything but that shape.

A brief snow squall told me I did not have all the time in the world to play with the canvas, as the edges lifted and flopped in the breeze. I jammed dirt clods against the outside edges to hold it in place. That is when my second best idea of the day came to me. Laying enough clods on it all 'round, I was able to keep the canvas in place. Then I layered more and more clods, cutting into the hillside behind the nest as I went. I figure the wind will come from the other direction most often, the north and east, so I dug into that slope.

It was tiring work but I managed to get enough dirt clods layered on the thing, right on top of the canvas. I don't mind saying that I began to get excited. It was shaping up to be stout, and the walls fairly thick. Inside I reckoned I could do as I wished with it, and I will. In fact, I might add dirt to the inside, too, depending on how much time and strength I have left.

But for now, though it is a misshapen thing, it is stout. Unless my poles suddenly give way with the weight of the clods, I suspect I have built something sturdy enough to protect me until Papa and the boys return. Perhaps other help will come in the meantime.

Beneath the dirt clods there is the layer of canvas. I do feel badly it has become so soiled, but I needed it and that is that. Beneath the canvas there is my frame of logs and poles and crosspieces woven with green boughs and anything else I could find that would bend. I decided to go up on the sides with clods only as high as I can reach. I am ashamed to say my strength isn't what it was, what with the cold and trying to preserve food.

The way the frame is built above that, there isn't much of a roof. It is not unlike a tipi, as we saw here and there on our journey. I recall thinking those Indians looked so very poor and miserable. Not a one of them did smile our way. I am quite certain I made up for this with my own grinning. Thomas told me I looked like the monkey in that book we used to own. At the time I wanted to box his ears, but now it seems a sweet-enough comment. I will save the ear-boxing for a later date.

At the top I was able to arrange the canvas so smoke from the stove will make its way once again up through its pipe and out the metal ring, as it had been in the wagon. It took no end of configuring, though. I don't know how it will be affected by snow. I dare say I will find out soon.

The space inside is not large, but it feels well insulated, or will, given all the sod I stacked and will continue to stack against the outside. It should hold heat well. At least better than the thin wood of the wagon.

I will cut pine boughs for the floor and arrange them so they will be fragrant and feel like cushions beneath my feet. That is my plan. As I have discovered lately, my plans don't always end up appearing as I intend them. I take comfort that I have accomplished what I set out to do so far. There is some satisfaction in that.

At this point in the construction of the nest, the day was aging, as Papa often calls late afternoon. So I began the long task of carrying to the nest everything I would need from the wagon. The first would be the stove.

I had not reckoned on how heavy that little steel pig really is. I made certain my fire from the morning tea was out and the stove cold, then I pulled apart the pipe and leaned it outside against the wagon. Not having canvas walls on the wagon was a blessing at this point as I could toss items right out between the arched wood ribs that look how I imagine a whale's bones might.

I managed to push and pull the stove to the end of the wagon. The tailgate was flopped down so I stagger-walked that stove to the back edge of the wagon and I set it down, but too far. It toppled with a godawful crash right to the ground. My heart wedged in my neck and I swear it stopped thudding for all of five seconds.

I jumped down beside the stove, expecting to find it cracked and broken and a smoke leaker far worse than it had been. But do you know what I found? It was fine, no damage at all. It helped that the ground is low and muddy there at the tailgate.

My next task was to move it the twenty feet to the slope, then down to the shelter. I took off the pieces that came apart easily—the lid and the door, which is on pin hinges. Then I bent to lift it, but found I could not. So I grabbed a bloody tarpaulin, folded it up, and rolled the stove onto it. Then I gathered the edges in my hand and dragged it backward. I found that by wedging my heels in the sloppy earth I was able to drag it several feet at a time. I tired right fast, though, and as I was nearly sitting on the ground after that last tug, I plopped down and rested.

I contemplated rolling it the rest of the way, but saw I was nearly to the top of the slope. That worried me. What if I could not slow it as it went down the slope? Surely such a rolling tumble would break the stove apart.

"Now, Janette," I said, for I have taken to talking out loud to myself. Papa always says you meet nicer people that way. "What you need to do is let the stove and canvas work for you." But how?

I walked around the contraption, and snapped my fingers. I had it. I pulled some of the tarp out from under itself so it was twice as big, then draped it over the stove. I grabbed the four corners, two to a hand, then I commenced to dragging again. It did not take long to reach the top of the slope.

Then as the weight of the stove nearly upset the apple cart, so to speak, I scrambled back around until I was on the upside of it. The weight of the stove kept pulling the bundle downslope, but I stayed upslope of it, jamming my heels in to slow it. In this manner we reached the bottom, me and the stove. Then came the hard part.

I made my door to the shelter quite high up on the wall, thinking it might be necessary should the snow build up. That storm had told me it would likely get deep. But how to get the stove all the way up there? I didn't think I could yarn it up there by tugging on the corners of the tarp.

Once again I had to set down and give it a think. This time I rested on the stove itself. I drummed on it with a hand wearing a holey sock. What to do?

It took another couple of minutes, but I am pleased to say I figured it out. I rolled the stove off the tarp, unfolded the bloodstained thing to its full size, and dragged one end inside the door. Then I climbed back out and down that bloodstained thing.

From the outside it looked like a great tongue sticking out of a tiny open mouth. I rolled the stove back onto the tarp. Then I grabbed the two corners, climbed over the little steel hog, and back inside. Once inside I pulled on the tarp, walking to the other side of the shelter. That didn't take but two strides.

I gathered more tarp and kept at it, each pull more difficult. Sure enough, it worked. Soon enough I saw the stove coming up to the hole as if it were peeking in at me.

"Hello, little stove. Welcome."

But that is about as far as the fun went, because I didn't have any idea how to get it inside and down to the floor. It was held in place by my own strength and my arms shook something fierce. I had to make a decision, and quick. So I gave the thing a mighty tug, then one more, and one more after that . . . and there was a second when I didn't feel any more pull from the stove and I said to myself, "Oh, Janette, this is all going to go badly."

But it didn't, other than the crash of the stove to the floor of my little shelter. It was dim in there, the only real light coming in from the top where the smoke hole was and from the doorway, neither hole of much size. But they shed enough light to let me know the little stove was muddy and messy but not broken.

I was steamed up by then, so I muckled onto it and managed to walk it like a crawfish over to the spot it needed to be. Close enough, anyway. I patted it, sat on it, and rested. Then climbed back out through that doorway and retrieved the rest of its parts. And that is the story of how the little stove made it from the wagon to the nest.

Of course, only after all that work did it come to me I could have avoided a whole lot of work if I had put more planning into the venture. I could have dragged that stove all the way down there before I built the nest. When I thought of that, I had a laugh. A real belly laugh like I'd not had in a month of Sundays.

I'd like to say the rest of it went smoothly, and for the most part it did, but I ran out of daylight and since I had to spend the night in the new shelter, there were more things to do on the list in my mind that I had time to do them. I was not able to cut pine boughs for the floor that first night, but I did arrange a trunk and two crates to serve as a bed of sorts. It would be a luxury to stretch out fully and sleep like God intended me to. I made sure the quilts all stayed off the muddy floor.

The larger items, such as the trunk, I had to empty and carry the innards down over many loads. I dared not leave anything up by the wagon that I could not bear losing or that might get soiled should we get snow in the night. What I could not bring, I covered with that grubby tarp. I prayed as I made my last load down to the nest that the critters would not be interested in it that night.

Turns out I ended up having to leave a fair number of goods up at the wagon, mostly spare tools, a second bucket, the wash basin, the larger of the two Dutch ovens—cooking for myself I have little need of the one I use, let alone two of them. They are items that will not be bothered by a little hard water (Papa's words for snow). I managed to cover them well enough with that tarp.

The most work I put into ferrying goods to the nest, after the heavy little stove, of course, was the salted meat. But I most definitely daren't leave that out for the critters. By now it gives off no scent of blood or meat smell that I am aware of. I know dogs, which must include wolves and coyotes and whatnot, can sniff much better than humans, but I did my best to cover it up well inside the nest.

Tuesday, October 30, 1849

Late yesterday afternoon, I was so cold and tired when I finished gathering wood that I decided I could do away with having to change out of those sweaty clothes. I should have known better. I did know better, and that is the thing of it. Today I awoke stiff and chilled to my marrow. I should not have neglected such a basic chore, and yet I did. Isn't that the way with people?

Thomas knew he should not stick his hands time and again in the jerky pouch, and yet he did just the same. It is as if each of us must see how much we can get away with in life. Always testing ourselves, our situations, thinking that one day we will find a better way to do a thing. Perhaps that is why people are the smartest of creatures. Then again perhaps we are not.

I do not know the answer, but I do know that from now on I will take care to lay out dry, if not warm, clothes to change into even if I am unable to bathe first. Anything would be preferable to how I feel as I write this.

I do not think much of heading out into the day, though it is a bright one with a blue sky overhead. That first snow caught me unawares and I can't let that happen again. So now, Janette girl, it is time to put down this pencil and once more make my way to the woods.

It is many hours later and the exertion of dragging more wood back to my nest was what I needed. I warmed up again and with it, I am afraid, I stank to high heavens, as Papa used to say when he'd return from scything or trudging behind Clem.

Though I am alone in this forsaken valley surrounded by mountains and little else, I do my best to keep my dignity when I am bathing. In truth, I long to peel off all these clothes and lie right down in a bath large enough to hold my entire body. Now wouldn't that be a luxury!

I must settle for heating water atop the stove and stripping off my shirt, blouse, undergarments, all the rest of it from the waist up, washing with a flannel wrung out in warm water. I start with my face, since the flannel is still clean and not yet smelling like sweat and little else. Then I pull on the layers of clothes I have hung up for the day to dry in the nest.

I tried putting damp clothes outside, but it is a rare day when the sun can do its job quicker than the cold air. I came back to the camp less than a week past and found shirts, socks, a dress, and a set of long underwear frozen stiff like planking. I was disappointed, but when I peeled them from the rock where I'd laid them out to dry in the sun but a few hours earlier, they retained their shape.

The longhandles reminded me of dancing with Thomas or William or Papa. Mostly Thomas because he loves to "step lively," as Papa calls it. Like Mama, he'd say.

William and Papa are similar peas sharing a pod, at least in that respect. They do very little to call attention to themselves. Though as a rule Will appears more lost in his own thoughts than Papa.

But on that day I danced around that camp, tired as I was, doing my best to remember the steps and calls of the square dances. Allemande left! Promenade! Do-si-do!

I laughed and I did not care who or what might be watching from behind a rock or tree or that cursed ridgeline. Let them watch. I was dancing.

Then the suit began to flop and bend in all the wrong places.

Soon it was as if I was holding a tired partner, and then just another piece of wet clothing. The red suit, long since faded to pink, matched my cheeks. "We must do this again, kind sir," I said, draping the longhandles to dry by the meager fire.

Since those clothes were still wet, I had to seek out others. Hauling wood, trying to build a snare for rabbits, and gathering pine cones and anything dry that might burn, I was soaked through all my layers. That was no way to hole up for the evening. So I rummaged in Will and Thomas's trunk. You will think it silly of me that I had not so much as peeked in there before, but it is the truth.

As I unstrapped the leather flaps buckling it closed and raised the flat wooden top, I fully expected to hear William or Thomas rush up behind me, shouting for me to get out, that I had no right to look in there. No right at all! I was a girl, those were their things, boy things.

I'd not raised the lid much at all when I thought thus, then came the knowledge they were not with me, would not be any time soon. I stopped my thoughts there, lest I give over to tears again. And that would be a waste of time, as I have well learned. In the next moment, as I creaked the lid higher, I smelled them, smelled their brother smell, wood smoke and lye soap and . . . something that cannot be put into words nor set on a page.

It is much too much of that. It is the smells of my brothers. And in that moment, as I tipped the box open, I was overcome with so much more feeling than I'd felt since the morning they left. The tears came readily and I did nothing to stop them. I buried my face in the sweet-smoky, soapy brother smells of their shirts, their tunics, their trousers, their long johns, their socks, their undergarments, and long minutes passed before I could stop myself.

And it was not that night that I could bring myself to wear their clothes. I stoked the fire and warmed a ragged, salty hunk of beef over flame. I ate it like an animal in a cave might, hunched in the flickering shadows, my face and hands feeling bare warmth from the small fire, my knees pulled up tight to my chin. And I felt good and sorry for myself for a long time that night until I fell asleep.

Friday, November 9, 1849

It has been a number of days since I wrote here in my journal. I'd like to say it bothers me not to write, but I have been so busy I didn't much think about it. I sometimes wonder why I am writing all this down, if I am truly the only one who will ever see it, and I hope that is the case, for I will keep it with me always. But what if . . . ? What if something should happen to me? Or what if nothing happens? The thought has been a constant visitor in my head.

As Papa says, the best way to get over a hurt you know is coming, or something that is plaguing you, is to get on with it, get it over with. So I will say the thing I don't want to think about, but that's busting to be told: I might never be found. I might never make my way to some place where people live. Any people, even Indians. Well, I don't know about Indians. But then again, if I do not know, then what's the harm in wondering?

If I am not found, my journal will rest with me for eternity. If I am found, I will have it with me, and at the end of my days I will have to determine what to do with it. If I am found, but I am dead, someone might well take the journal and . . . what? What is the worst they could do with it? Read it? Would I care? Not a whit at that point, as I will be, as Papa says of the deer and squirrels he kills, past the point of caring.

Enough of this maudlin thinking. I will go back over what has happened to me since I last wrote so many days ago. These have been some of the busiest days of my entire life, mostly for the chores I must keep up with daily—checking on my food, adding to my supply of wood, making sure the wagon cover is fastened down 'round the outside of the nest, washing myself, washing clothes, checking for footprints of creatures and trying to figure out what they might have been that visited me in the night. Rather those I heard prowling outside. Visiting is too friendly a word for what I believe they had in mind.

To a wolf or lion or bear I am a toothsome treat, nothing more, nothing less. But to something smaller, say a rabbit, I am the one who views it as food. That is the way of the world, so says Papa. And while I know that to be true, it is doubly painful when you have to kill to survive. Killing in battle, I imagine, is easier than killing something to eat. If Papa could read this now, he would be worried I might be turning soft.

I am not soft, but neither am I hard-hearted. It is my concern about running out of food that drove me to fashion snares to catch the rabbits. I saw the tracks and the droppings, so I knew I had such visitors, and not too far from camp. I also know how to skin a rabbit. But I am getting ahead of myself.

I saw what a fine sky I had been presented with, so I decided to venture afield, dressed warmly and armed with the shotgun and a hip knife. The day was a bright one and the sky extra blue, but all that means to me, given that it is November and given where I am located, is that I would be cold sooner each day, once the sun begins its slow slide down the river valley.

I set off upstream with a light heart, hoping for some luck to help me find a rabbit. In my mind I could taste Mama's stewed rabbit, smell the warm, thick odors that filled the kitchen of our old home. Where did they all go—those long-ago, far-off days and their people? Nowhere to be seen, I told myself.

I kept on walking, lugging my supplies. I scanned for sign and found a track a few days old. Nothing fresh. But then I'd only been out very far from camp a few times. I looked around myself.

To the north, snow lay draped like clean linen over the great gray jags of stone of the mountains. I shuddered and moved on. I have been alone for a month and nearly two weeks, and have spent much of my time in these woods. I have learned to move slowly, take but three or four steps, then stop. I look around, moving only my eyes, then slowly turn my head.

I am not sure if this is how one must hunt, because Papa never took me hunting, but it appears to be what the animals do. I watched a deer, different than the ones we had back home. Ours were whitetails. Here, they appear mostly to be what I call blacktails. They look like the white tails, but they are larger and thicker. They also have black hair on their backsides. But what concerns me most is how they act.

They walk so silently into a place. I can be watching the meadow near the camp, thinking of nothing and everything, all at once, and then there will be deer, one, two, or five, not but eighty feet before me. Right there. And I watch them, partly because they are so gentle that having them close by makes me feel reassured somehow. As if I had friends not far away. I know that sounds silly, but it's true. And as it's my journal, I don't care what anyone else may think on the matter.

They walk forward, nearly as a group. Though they are scattered, there is a way they go about this, with some of the group looking behind them while others dip their heads down to paw at the snowpack to get at the grasses beneath. They sample all the bramble plants and leafless branches around the edge of the field, but they are always looking, slowly walking. They rarely take a step forward that they don't match with a held step, looking all around themselves. Their eyes are on the sides of their heads, Papa pointed out to me one day on a deer he had shot. That way they can see in more than one place at a time.

"How come humans can only see forward?" I recall asking him.

He looked at the deer, looked at me, pushed his hat back on his forehead and said, "I reckon it's because we have to figure out other ways to defend ourselves. We are not often the ones who are pursued, but we are often the ones doing the pursuing." He brought the end of a long finger to that space at the top of his long nose, between his eyes. "And for that," he said, "we mostly need to look forward."

Now that I am in a position of being both the pursued and the pursuer, I believe Papa is mostly right on that account. Though I don't know if he has ever been pursued. Mama once told me he fought in skirmishes he did not talk about. Perhaps men pursued him, tried to run him aground like an animal. My mind had better stop this terrible thinking right now.

I stood in the woods, past the place in the trees I marked in my mind as the boundary where I feel safe. That is the lone boulder half covered with mosses that shone in the sun even this late in the year as a whole mix-up of shades of green. I stood my ground, held my gun crosswise before me, as Papa showed me, ready to swing it up should I see something I could eat or that might take a fancy to eat me. Either way, I hoped I would get off a shot before I lost out.

Other than the high-up hushing sound of the wind in the tops of the tall pines, there was precious little commotion. I was aware of a woodpecker rapping his beak somewhere not far off. To the northwest, a songbird, likely a thrush, was searching for another. I notice songbirds favor sunlight, so hearing him didn't disrupt me much.

I was fixing to move as the deer, so after my good look-see around the place I lifted my left boot and was about to step forward. I was careful to look toward the ground, patches of bare earth with sparse snow deep in the trees. I looked for sticks and twigs that might snap underfoot. As I lifted my foot something huge and covered in black hair moved from out of the darkest part of the woods, right where I was headed.

I would not have seen it had I not been glancing up from where I wanted to set my foot down. That thing did not make a sound as it moved. It stepped away from the darkness and then I saw it was not black but brown-black, as an arm of sunlight angling through the trees lit a strip of fur like momentary fire. Another did the same as it shuffled forward.

The light laid slowly across its face—the blunt snout, the dark, wide-apart pig eyes, ears so small they almost were not there. It was a bear. As it moved, looking as if it were on a Sunday walk, it swung its head from one side to the other, slow as you please, its black nose curving and sniffing all on its own.

Its big, wagging shoulders reminded me for all the world like those of a buffalo, only with a hump that wagged as it walked. But this was no buffalo. I knew it was a grizzly bear, as Papa had pointed them out to me and the boys a number of times on the trail. We'd only ever had black bears at home. As I stood there with my heart frozen like a winter stone in my chest, I recalled something else Papa said about them. You cannot outrun them.

I had very little in the way of wits about me, though I remembered he also said they have poor eyesight, but they can by gum work those sniffers of theirs. A grizzly will pick up a scent of a rabbit or ripe berries from a great, long distance.

As if he was whispering in my ear, I heard more of Papa's advice about grizzly bears echo in my rabbity mind: "Pray the wind is at your face if the thing's in front of you. Then it won't smell much of you and you might be able to stand stock-still. And maybe, just maybe you'll be passed by."

I did that, though I had no idea where the wind was coming from—front, back, or sides. For all I knew at that moment it was headed straight down from heaven on high. I'd like to say I bested that great beast, but the truth is I am one lucky girl, Papa. I stood stock-still because I don't think I could have recalled how to work that great booming gun you left me with, even if I had to.

The bear kept on walking, not toward me, I saw with great relief, but angling off to my left, southeastward. Toward camp. That was another thing I decided I'd worry about later. At the moment all I wanted to do was not make a squeak or a peep, not dare to breathe . . . though of course I had to breathe, and my breaths went in and out in tiny puffs. And that is what nearly got me ripped apart as I stood there imitating a foolish deer.

You will recall I said my left foot was all but lifted and ready to set down again. Well, while I watched the bear and hoped he wasn't watching me, I had been mostly balanced. But mostly is not all the way, and I finally had to let my breath out. The bear was not but sixty feet or so away from me, snuffling and taking his sweet time to cross through the pine grove, his massive feet padding one after the other. The nails were great long raking tools like the hand cultivator we used on the garden back home, waggling every time he set a foot down again.

And speaking of feet, my left foot needed more pressure on it lest I topple. I did my best to shift weight to even out, but it did not work that way.

When I eased that cursed foot down again something under it, a baby of a twig, snapped. I barely heard it, so small and muffled was it beneath my boot. But that bear heard it. He stopped, like the deer in the meadow, and swung that big head so he was looking straight at me. Oh Lord, but that jellied me inside.

I stood frozen, but soon enough, cold drops of fear-sweat rolled down my face. I prayed for them to stop sliding down my nose, my eyes, out from under my woolen knitted cap, but they kept right on rolling. The gun was heavier with each second that passed. The sack I'd slung over my right shoulder felt as if it wanted to slide off and spill my poorly made snare parts right at my feet, like an invitation to the big bear to come on over for dinner.

His big, staring face was wide, now that I saw it full-on. Wide and with hair all blooming out of it, like when you stare into the middle of a sunflower. Only this was no sunflower. That big black nose worked in all directions harder than ever, begging for a slip of a scent of whatever it was that made that noise.

Its ears were bigger than I had seen before, but only because they were pricked up and cupped in my direction. The eyes, though, Papa, were like you said. He sort of squinted and tried to draw a sight on me, like it was unsure of what it saw. But that nose was working, and the ears twitched all the time.

My sweat droplets kept rolling and the gun was a heavier thing with each passing second. The bear's mouth parted slightly with shallow breaths. Its black lips sagged like played-out leather strapping, and I saw big yellow teeth that could do terrible things to my body. My left leg shook, and I prayed it didn't jiggle enough to move my skirts. My hands gripped that shotgun tight but they were about to commence with the shakes, too.

My heart sorted out what it was meant for, and began to thump something fierce, as if to make up for being scared to a stop. If the bear didn't do something soon, I would shiver all over and give myself away.

I forced my mind to remember how to work the gun. It would be my only chance. Papa, you said you can't outrun a bear, and seeing that big beast, I knew you were right. Something about it was powerful and convincing. Seeing it staring at me, but not at me, if that makes sense, chilled me more than any dunk in a frozen river. It convinced me it was king of all these mountains, and I sincerely hoped I was another meal for another time.

Even writing that now, three days after the fact, makes my hands shake. I have to stop for now. It is late and I have spent too much time today in my own mind, as Papa has often accused me of.

Saturday, November 10, 1849

Remember how I mentioned I had three days that were frightening and overwhelming? I may not have used those exact words, but believe me, seeing the bear was only the beginning. I'd like to say it got better, but it didn't. I stood that way, not moving, or trying not to, anyway. Much as I wanted to look like a tree or a rock, I am not one. I am a girl, and my legs shook and my hands shook and I kept right on sweating cold, stinging sweat in my eyes. Still, I stayed like that as long as I could.

By the end, I was trembling so bad I looked like old Mimsy from the next farm over, before she died. She shook with what Papa called "her palsy." I wanted to laugh at myself, even if that bear was still out there somewhere.

Finally after what I am sure was much of an hour, I decided I had to move. With intention, that is. My body had already decided to move on its own sometime before that. I told myself all at once I was going to drop down to one knee and at the same time pull the stock of that big gun right up to my shoulder. I would thumb the hammers back, and be ready should that big bear still be there, out of sight, trying to decide if I was something to eat or something to ignore. That's what I told myself, anyway. What really happened was that I fell over. More to the point, I collapsed.

If that shotgun had been on cock, I would have blown myself apart, or blown a big ol' hole in the ground right at my feet. But all I did was drop. I tried to scramble up to that kneeling position I could see in my mind, but my body wanted nothing to do with it.

I finally managed to get my right foot planted firm, and shoved myself up to a sitting position. I yarned on that shotgun, but for the life of me I could not raise it more than a few inches from my lap. I let it sag back down, rubbed a hand across my soggy eyes and pushed my hat back off my forehead. I had sweated enough for two people. You would have thought I'd been chopping firewood for hours.

My heart came back to itself, too, and my body told me I should rest. So I did, sat right there and did nothing for a few minutes. But I kept a watchful eye. That bear had made hardly any sound at all. That was the most frightening part. I could have walked right up to him without even knowing it.

Then a thought came to me. Papa said that bears go to sleep all winter. They den up and don't come out until the snow melts and finds its way down to the rivers and the grasses poke their heads up, looking for sunlight.

So why wasn't this bear asleep? Maybe Papa was wrong, though I don't think so. Likely this bear was late in heading to his den, looking to curl up and sleep away the long winter.

That's about what I wanted to do, too. And my thoughts turned to the camp. If that big grizzly kept walking in the direction I saw him head, he'd tromp smack-dab into my nest. That's when I realized no matter how solid I make my nest, now that I'd seen a grizzly bear up close, there was no way on the good earth it could hold up to a bear looking for food or a place to sleep the winter through.

I made tracks for camp. I was careful to swing wide to the north, so as to spy on it from across the meadow. All I could think as I made my cautious way out of the woods was my meat cache. If that bear got into it, I would be in sorry shape.

It hadn't much occurred to me I will need to safeguard the

camp while I am gone. How do I go about that? I will have to figure it out right quick if bears are roving during the daytime while I am off cutting wood or trying to snare rabbits.

A rock of fear in my belly burned hotter with each step closer to camp. Then I made it out from the edge of the woods and into the little meadow. It is now mostly a rumpled quilt of white with rocks and knobs of brown, dried grasses stitching the place together in odd patterns. The camp was off to my right, hard by the river. I kept walking as I looked that way, expecting to see a big brown-black beast standing up on its rear legs, swatting my little nest apart.

I slowed, stopped, my breath gasping out of me. It's harder to breathe in the mountains, and I tire sooner than I ought. I held a hand over my eyes and squinted. The sun was behind me. I turned, angling my sight line once more toward the camp, and saw nothing I did not want to see.

That was good. I admit I feel the nervous flutters whenever I return to camp. It is that time before I know for certain nothing's changed, when it's a possibility I still might see Papa. He'll have a hand over his eyes looking right back at me, my brothers to either side of him. And he'll see me at the same time I see him. Oh, writing that makes me so happy, and then, as quick, I am alone once more.

I have to stay strong, take care of myself and the camp, so they might see the smoke or smell it. That will be the happiest day of my life, and I am looking forward to it.

But about the bear. Even though I did not see the bear anywhere near camp doesn't mean it wasn't hidden, sniffing and pawing my goods. I cut a wide circle around the camp, so as to see around the river side of the nest. It took me longer than I expected.

I stopped, eyed the camp. I threw caution to the breeze and made for it. Didn't take me long to reach the wagon. I was sure there was no bear near it because I saw through the ribs and under it. Unless that ol' bear was lying down in the wagon, stretched out and snoozing like Thomas of an afternoon back home under the crab apple tree.

The nest is beyond that, positioned between the wagon and the river, along the berm I used to help make the wall. I rested a hand on the wagon, solid and comforting. I made my way around the end, stepping slow, hoping there wasn't anything on the ground under the thin snowpack that might give me away.

With each step closer to the nest my heart bumped and thumped louder in my chest, so loud at times I swear if a bear was about he would have heard it, too. Soon enough I was at a spot where I saw most of the way around my little winter shelter. It all looked as I'd left it.

I let out my breath in a long, nervous sort of way and lowered the gun for what I hoped was the last time that day. I was tuckered. I held it loose in my left hand, and made my way down the dug-in steps I'd cut into the hillside. They lead at an angle to a wide space before my front door. I have tried to make it homey, but it is a low sort of spot. I still mean to gather needled boughs to lay there so I won't have to stomp through mud each time I go out or in.

I was about to step up onto the rock I'd worried into place. It helps me get height to climb into the door I made, which is four or more feet up off the ground, and I reckon that helps keep me a little safer.

I looked down to see where to set the butt of the gun when my eye caught something below me. Pressed into the snowy mud, right beside where I'd stepped, was a huge paw print. I stopped breathing again. I hope that isn't about to become a habit.

I stared at the print, water still pooling and oozing in the cratered center. There were puckers where the claws had set, then pushed off again, smearing the mud and creaming it into the snow. There was another track, and another.

Soon I saw at least two dozen bear prints, right where I was standing. Judging from the direction the prints pointed, it had been sniffing at my nest walls, at the mud and weed-packed sides. I wanted to jump through the door and hide myself inside. But then I got the silly notion into my head that the bear had somehow figured out how to get into my house. I finally mustered enough bravery to peek in, but it was too dark in there to do much more than squint and wonder what shape was what.

Eventually I grew too tired to let my mind play its tricks on me, so I climbed on into the nest. Before I closed the door, I looked out around the campsite, certain I would see the bear peeking at me from the other side of the shelter. But no. At least not that night.

WEDNESDAY, NOVEMBER 14, 1849

I woke in the nest in the dark of the cold, still night. I was stiff. Something, a sound outside, had awakened me. I did not move. It was footsteps, and my heart sounded like far-off cannon fire in my chest. In that moment, I knew it was Papa, that he'd finally made his way back to me. And there were other sounds, too. The boys!

I was set to call out when my happiness was taken from me. Outside the nest wall of canvas and earth, I heard something sniffing. Whatever was nosing around out there could not have been any more fearsome than the creature I conjured in my cursed mind.

I pictured it taller than the nest, and with matted fur and crusted sores, the cause of which I know not. And its great, black, wet nose worked almost as if it were a beast all its own, twitching this way and that, before finally settling on my scent. Then its mouth dropped open beneath the snout and a scarred pink tongue slopped and dangled and drooled over too many rows of meat-choked fangs, curved and snapped and as raw and jagged as the mountains all about my little valley.

But this was not what was out there, could not be. It did not grunt how I imagined a bear might. It snuffled like a pig. No, it was more like a . . . dog. And that's when I knew it had to be a coyote or a wolf. It sounded like Belle, our old hound, when she was on the scent of something and didn't want to let up, her snout making a sort of coughing-chuckling sound. It snuffled closer and I heard my heart pounding like what I imagine an Indian war drum sounded like. I felt the pounding in my neck, all the way up my throat, even in my nose.

How was I to live through this? Where was the gun? I had leaned it too far from me in the dark. I swear, sometimes I don't have the sense of a goose. At least I had the big knife with me. It lay close by my hand and I groped for it with my fingers. The cold bone handle, the bent steel hilt, the stiff leather sheath all felt reassuring.

I pulled at it with my fingertips and the knife slid on the quilt, the slightest of sounds ever made, but the snuffling, two beasts at it now, and not but a few feet from me, stopped. Dead still.

I didn't dare breathe. I fancy the unmistakable stink of wet dog reached my nose as I sat huddled in blankets. There was the rank tang of hair and sweat and something else I had never smelled. Somehow I knew what it was—it was wildness. It was far from the way people live. And it made me not want to take another breath. Made me want to become smaller and smaller until I could fit between clumps of frozen mud and worm my way deep in the earth.

With no warning one of the beasts howled a long, loud cry, ragged at the edges as if it had been howling all day long and had grown hoarse. The cry dragged out of it as if pulled against its will, tapering to a quavering, trembling sound. Wolves.

I jerked in my blankets, which I had wrapped beneath my boot heels. The beasts did not hear me. I jammed a wad of Mama's quilt in my mouth, tasted the spongy cotton and smelled the smoke of a hundred and more campfires that gets into everything. I bit down hard, stifling the scream that wanted to climb out of my throat.

I tasted blood. I had bit the inside of my mouth, and I did not care. That wash of fear was the beginning of a long night. I knew I had to keep awake. Within minutes of the wolf's howl, I heard the soft thumping of others drawing closer, racing toward the nest.

I breathed hard through my nose, not daring to let my mouth have the chance to scream, to reveal to the wolves there was someone, some *thing* inside. Could they make it into the nest? Yes, my mind told me. They will dig down to you and fill this sad little hovel and you will have nowhere to go.

It kept up like that for an hour, perhaps longer. Then, as quickly as they had come, my tormenters vanished, one by one, trotting off to some other distraction. But I have no doubt they will return. They know I am here. They smelled me.

THURSDAY, NOVEMBER 22, 1849

It is my birthday, or near enough—I curse myself each day for neglecting diligence with the calendar. My diary entries well could be off by several days, or perhaps a week, though I hope they are at least consistent with each other. Since today is bright and promising with blue skies and a warm breeze, I choose to believe my birthday is this fine day. I allowed myself a cry. Tomorrow I shall not.

I indulged in something special and cooked an extra half portion of beefsteak and johnnycake. I long for milk and eggs, but made do with water in the cornmeal. I even managed to coax a sprinkling of pepper from Papa's grinder, which I thought had been emptied sometime before.

It is days such as this I wish I had taken up a musical instrument. Mama was the musical one in the family. The rest of us can carry a tune well enough, but she played her spinet for church meetings and often at night. It was a lovely sound and now that I write this I find myself longing for another good cry.

I am sorry, Mama. I should have not been so stubborn, should not have been the girl who wanted to be out in the fields with Papa instead of in the house with you. I should have said, "Yes, ma'am, a thousand times yes, I will learn to play the spinet, but only if you will teach me."

I say this to you now, but other than the brief sunshine and a raven sawtoothing away from here—oh luckiest of birds!—I am alone. No one hears me when I cry or sing.

Since my birthday is in late November, the twenty-second, to be precise, that means many months of winter ahead. I pour hot water in the last of Mama's teacups and look at the pretty blue flowers until it is too dark to see them. Happy Birthday, Janette.

DECEMBER (EARLY?), 1849

My visitor has come. Likely the worst of all.

Cramping woke me, deep in my gut, like a tiny fist covered in apple thorns, twisting and twisting without cease. I thought at first it might be the beef.

A moment of dread filled me, for I suspected that if I had salted it wrongly, then surely I was doomed. I have no other food, nor a practical firearm to "make meat," as Papa calls it, save the shotgun. And precious little education regarding that brute of a weapon. Why should Papa have taught me to use a shotgun? Why should he not have? Because I am a girl? That notion sets my jaw tight, as always.

But all worry of food came to naught, shadowed instead by the bigger worry of my visitor. I have experienced unseen visitors before, many times, in fact, since I built this little snow-covered hovel. But always they are toothy and hairy and snarling and hungry and secretive. But none so devious and unseen as this.

I long for you, Mama. For your cool touch on my forehead. Your hands, I recall, were not soft, but hardworking with red knuckles and calluses. But I miss them all the same. You should be here now, for me. I need your help.

I am using one of Thomas's shirts, it being in the worst condition, despite my many mendings. It is stitched by me in a dozen places, tiny precise lines like the tracks of a railway. The blue thread runs up and down the sleeves, the back, one side—each repair marking a time on the trail when he had gotten himself stuck on something and in anger pulled himself free, making work for me.

And now that shirt has come to this, a stopper for this unseen, unwanted visitor that hurts me from the inside out. I believe I know enough about it to deal with it, nothing more.

I am not so ignorant of the way a woman's body functions, yet my first thought on waking and finding myself sticky with blood was that I had been attacked in the night by some animal still hiding in a dark corner of this nest. The truth came quickly to me, yet my waking thought did haunt me for long minutes even as I took stock and figured a way to meet this new task.

And that led me to the most frightening thought of all—what shall I do with the soiled cloths? They will no doubt carry a more pungent scent than I am able to detect. And that means animals, the lions and wolves, will be drawn to my camp more than ever.

Not for the last time do I wonder why I had the misfortune to be born a girl. I am tired writing this and my day has just begun.

DECEMBER ?, 1849

I have done what I vowed to myself I would not do. (And who else would I vow to?) I read over what I wrote three days before today. It was a Saturday, I think. In truth I have muddled the days of the week. My method of keeping track was to be a simple one, a notch for each day, cut in the stick I fashioned from a stout branch for this purpose.

I used Papa's skinning knife, careful to nick only the rod and not my own hand. Where would that leave me? A wound in this vast place? Bah, one notion leads to another. Back to my first thought. I reread what I wrote days before, something I try not to do. It is so muddled, little more than a waste of paper and effort.

Later the same day and it is so cold, I cannot continue to fritter words nor ink nor pencil nor the breath it takes to warm my fingers. I daren't leave them long outside my mittens.

There is one finger, the one that points on my left hand, or more to the point, ha ha, it has gone a dark shade of violet, like a bruise. Though I prefer to think of it as one of the many colors that make up a sunset. A pretty one, though, as in summertime, when it is still warm, so warm, that only the lightest of clothes are necessary. The finger does not like to move when I tell it to. This is troublesome. I have heard tell of people losing parts of themselves to the cold. If ever there was a person in danger of this, it is me.

I have nothing more to say tonight. Except that soon, the

cold wind will become padding, scuffing feet. And they will become grunting breaths that become that devil of a wolf or whatever it is my mind conjures.

Then I will sleep no more until morning, when there will be too much to do—fetch wood for the fire, as that is all there is to do. Unless I can make up some housekeeping. Yes, that will be a good thing to think about while I try to sleep. Any sleep will be welcome before the wolf in my mind won't let me. Mama, I need you here. I will think on you instead of housekeeping.

Late December, 1849

I am certain that Christmas has come and gone. I always enjoyed it, but the thought of it now saddens me so, I cannot even think of it, let alone write of it. When I think of you all, Mama and Papa and William and Thomas, I am heartsick. You are somewhere, all of you, without me. And I am here, without you. It is too much and I fear it will never become less so.

January ?, 1850

It is a new year, must be by now, and I hate being in here, in this dark, cramped, smoke-filled hovel. And yet I find myself not wanting to leave it. For when I force my way through the many safeguards I have set up, when I crawl up through the snow to the surface my head will be swiped clean from my shoulders. It will be a bear or a lion or a wolf or some other beast no one in the world has ever seen, except me. But as it will be the very last thing I see, it will not matter so much.

January, 1850

I dreamed last night of Calbert Bentley. I call him Cal because I have never liked the name Calbert. Sounds like someone with a long neck whose teeth are so far-spaced he could eat corn through a picket fence. That's one of Papa's not-so-kind comments, but he mostly keeps them to himself.

Of all the people I could spend my time dreaming of, it is funny that he should come to mind. But I've come to realize that when it's asleep, the mind is a curious thing. My dreams here are all one way or all the other—exciting and pleasant or dark and filled with unspoken things that make me fearful of going back to sleep. But the dream of Cal was a good one. It should be, as he flattered me like no other.

I have not written about him before now because I have forced myself to think of other things when his face came to mind. He was a handsome boy. I say was because I doubt I shall ever see him again.

As with the farm and Mama's grave, my thoughts of him are best tucked away, and if not forgotten then certainly laid in the hope chest in my mind. It is the one with all the memories of Mama. And of other moments, such as that time I was alone at the pond, and saw the baby ducks. One of them mistook me for its own mama.

It came so close I touched its wee downy back with one finger, then its real mama called. Before it paddled away, it looked at me, and I swear it looked confused. I think I was, too, for a moment.

That's where my mind's portrait of Cal Bentley has been, until last night. He came unbidden into my dream and everything that happened that Saturday afternoon in late May happened all over again.

In my dream we knew we would be staying on the farm forever (that is the caution of dreams, they are far too safe and tidy). This time when Cal stood by the oak along what we called Teacher's Lane, which leads back to school and church and town, he looked as if he had been waiting on me forever and would have kept on waiting, even if I never happened along.

But in my dream I had come along, and I was happy to see him. That is about all there was to it. The feeling was a nice one, and we were two happy people. What really happened that day has stayed with me, as if I experience it over and over for the first time. And it still leaves me feeling torn in two.

I had known Cal for a long time, nearly all my life, and had always paid him little heed. He was always there, someone to josh with at the schoolyard, that sort of thing. But on that day in late May, I was walking back home from the mercantile where I'd gone to fetch cinnamon sticks for baking, and leather scraps and a tack needle for Papa. Clem's patch-covered harness was in need of another mending. In truth it was more mend than collar, but Papa is always talking about making things wear out before you give up on them. That is sound thinking.

I spied Cal from a long way off as I walked down the road. I took my time, figuring he'd walk with me the rest of the way, at least to his parents' farm. He looked odd, sort of leaning against the tree but not really leaning, like he was trying too hard to lean. It made more sense then, so you'll have to take my word for it. And since I am the one who will read this, I reckon I'll know what I meant. Bah!

I should have known something was off right then and there.

But I can be thick in the bean at times, as Papa says of Thomas, before he pats him on the head like he's a confused puppy.

The closer I walked toward Cal, the more jittery he got. I swear it was like watching someone who knows he's about to catch what for when he's done something bad. And then I recalled all the times he had joined Thomas in calling me Miss Prim and pinching the back of my arm in class—they gave me purple welts—so I slowed down.

I finally wandered up alongside the tree and stopped, shifted the straps of my tote sack to my other shoulder. "Cal Bentley, what on earth are you up to? Seems to me you ought to have better things to do than stand beside a dusty road looking all fidgety."

He stepped down off the roadside out from under the shade of the tree. Then he took off his hat! I was about to tell him he needed to have his hair tended to—it was spidery and too long. He worked that brim between his hands, round and round, getting nowhere except in circles.

"Put that hat back on your head, Cal. Blonde as you are you'll get a sunburn right quick."

He looked at the hat as if wondering how it came to be in his hands. "Oh, oh yes," he said, but he still didn't put it on his head.

That's when I knew for certain something wasn't right with him. I stopped funning him. "Cal, is something wrong? Are your folks ill?"

"No, no, nothing like that . . . Janette. I was hoping . . ." Then he went silent again, looked back toward the tree, at the road, toward the hills behind me, anywhere but at me.

"Cal Bentley, I don't understand what it is you're up to, but you're acting like Thomas, and even he doesn't act so squirly most of the time."

"Janette," he said again, swallowed, then moved another step closer.

He was still a good arm's length away. Right then he looked taller to me. I hadn't seen him in a month or more, come to think on it. He'd been busy planting with his pa and uncles, not in school much. But there he was, grown bigger somehow, like his shirts didn't fit him so well over the shoulders.

I noticed such things because I had to add gussets to Will's shirts as he grew to be a young man. And then it dawned on me that's what was happening to Cal. He was growing up. I had always been taller than him, now I never would be again. And it hadn't taken long.

He cleared his throat. I'll give him this much, he tried to look me in the eyes, but the sun was behind me, so I think that's what made it difficult for him. When he finally started talking, his words came out fast, each new word stomping on the one before it. I had a time following him for a few seconds.

"Janette . . . I've been meaning to ask you something. Only I need to talk with you before I can talk with your father."

"My papa? Why, Cal, if you want to talk with Papa, just—"

"No, I mean I, aw." He smacked his hat against his leg. "Hang fire, Janette, I only wanted to know if you wouldn't be too offended if I came to call on you one day soon."

"Call on me? Why, whatever for, Cal?" And do you know, at that very moment, I still didn't understand what he was asking me. But as I watched his face redden even deeper, like a hammer-struck thumb, and saw his blue eyes sort of lose their shine, that's when I understood what he was on about. And then it was my turn to go all red in the face.

I saw what he found so interesting in the dirt road at our bare feet. And when I was in mid-blush and about to say something to encourage him, I felt the weight of the burlap satchel on my shoulder, and I remembered the trip west. I knew

I had no right to plant seeds of hope in Cal's mind. That would be unfair.

Now I realize that what I said next was even more unfair. I should have told him we were leaving. We hadn't told many people at all, though I assumed he would have heard. Everyone always knew their neighbors' business, anyway.

"I'm sorry, Cal. I . . . I don't think that would be a good idea."

And that was it, that was all I said to him. Like a shame-faced child I hugged that bag tight to my belly and walked fast all the way home without once looking back. I spent the time jumping back and forth from one feeling to another.

Firstly, I was angry with Papa for making us go. Then at myself for being so foolish in front of Cal. Then at the sky for being such a pretty blue on such a horrible day. Then at the sparrow hawk flapping then falling like a dropped stone to snatch up some poor field mouse.

The next moment my guts felt like a ball of snakes writhing around at the thought that Cal Bentley wanted to pay a social call on me. On me? Me! The way he reddened and lacked for words, he wasn't funning me.

Blonde, blue-eyed Cal, whose father was a farmer and wheelwright and mother was always so kindly, though she often came down with the vapors—Papa always smiled when he said that. Cal, who I had known forever and a day, Cal who had got-ten taller and older-looking since I last saw him. Or at least since I last paid attention to him. Had I ever?

And now, as I write this in my journal, sitting in the doorway of my nest, somewhere in the Rocky Mountains, not yet to Oregon, not anywhere I know by name, alone and nothing but alone, now when it is far too late, I find myself thinking about Cal. I wonder if he ever thinks of me.

The last time I saw him was the morning we left. He stood

beside his parents. I had already climbed up into the wagon. There were perhaps a dozen people there to wave us off, not including Cousin Merdin and his brood.

Right then I wished for Cal to run to the wagon and tell Papa no, no, this is not right, tell him he needed to speak with him. And part of me said no, that would not be right, don't let it happen.

My second wish was the stronger one. And I hate that. Not because now I am alone, but because when it came down to it, neither Cal nor I had the courage to do anything more than offer a weak wave to each other. We were two people who had been friends our entire lives. Surely that held some meaning, some importance to us. But it did not.

He turned away east to his parents' farm, and I turned in my seat and faced west, not looking back. Like that day I left him standing in the road, his old brown felt hat in his hand, and his clean shirt and messy yellow hair. And those pretty blue eyes.

He had the courage then to hint at what he had in mind, his deepest thoughts about me. And I had the courage, I see now, to do what I thought was right. But knowing that didn't make it easy then, and it doesn't make me feel any better now.

January ?, 1850

Yesterday, a break in the cutting wind and pellets of ice filled me with boldness. I ventured further away from camp than I had since my second day here. I wonder if I would have been better off had I been lost then. Such speculation is a fool's game, still I get up to it far too often for my own good. Perhaps I am a fool. Who is to debate the issue with me? The crows? The mice? The wolves? The wind? These cursed mountains?

What I was thinking yesterday, I will never know. I blame the weather and my need to stretch my legs. The nest may well be snug, but it is also dark and small and stifling. And if I am to be honest, it smells bad, like the cave of an animal. Which is fair, for that is what I am at present.

I am an animal in a dark hole in the earth, with all my sweated-up clothes, the socks and boots offending the worst. Save, perhaps, for the stink of meat always on the edge of greening, or the off scent of burnt fat dribbling and mixing with the sharpness of wood smoke.

Smoke curls its way into everything, the cold clouding of my own stale breath, the low stink of my thunder pot, though I empty it each morning well away from the nest. And there is the ground beneath it all that I long ago gave up on keeping clean with fresh boughs. They have since been worked into the churn of frozen muck beneath my booted feet.

I do my best each day to air it, to clean what I am able, but the daylight hours are short and my strength has ebbed in keeping with the thinning of my arms and legs.

"Weight is all," Papa had said when loading the wagon. "We will be able to replenish our supplies, first at small-town mercantiles, then as we roll westward, at trading posts, where we will purchase the goods we cannot shoot or gather. But if we were to load the wagon at the outset with all the food-stuffs we would need, especially with your brothers' appetites"— here I recall Papa's eyebrows rising as if he had learned he had come into a vast fortune—"why, the poor team would never be able to pull the wagon a dozen feet, let alone thousands of miles."

And that is why we had barely enough dried beans, coffee, cornmeal, flour, and sugar by the time we stopped in these mountains. Papa reckoned we were not many more weeks' travel from the place we sought. I am the one who has paid for that judgment.

It is the dank hole in which I live, and my need to crawl up and out of it at every opportunity to see the light of day and feel the snow crunch beneath my boots that drove me out along a path I had not followed much beyond the edge of my wood-gathering place. But yesterday I did.

The light, though gray, was plentiful, the hour early, and the air cold enough to brace me, but not so frigid it hurt my lungs to take it in. Most days lately have not been like that, so I indulge in outings when I can.

I deliberated on whether to take along the shotgun, and decided I had better. There is always the chance I will spot something worth shooting, or at least I might frighten off a menacing critter. Had I known the truth in that, I would have stayed put, stink or no.

The trail is little more than a sightline I stick to. But I commit to memory waypoints I know will lead me back to camp should a sudden storm fill in my boot tracks. Since much of this place is sparsely treed, I mark my route with thin branches and dried grasses as long as my arm that I stick upright in the snow every little while. In the trees I snap branches, but as that is how I also gather my tinder sticks, there is little point in marking a trail in such a manner.

For a long time I dithered on hacking a slash mark in tree bark with the knife. I imagined the trees react much the same as I would were someone to cut on my legs with a blade! But the thought of perishing in a squall within trekking distance of my nest gave me pause.

I now make two cuts in tree bark. One straight in, at chest height—high enough, I hope, to surmount the height of the winter's snow—and another downward thrust to meet the first. In that manner I am able to make a simple two-cut blaze on a tree. Sometimes it takes me three. I always hold my breath whilst I cut, and then I apologize to the tree.

Back to my breathy tale. (It is worth it provided my pencil holds out!)

It was slow going, even though I stuck to the stretches of snow where the wind keeps it thin on the ground. In this manner I picked my way along, circling, then climbing in a left-to-right fashion up a rocky hillside.

It is curious, but when you live in one place for any length of time you come to think it is the whole of the world. That knobby slope is not far from camp, but I had not laid eyes on it.

Pine trees of some sort jutted from it like bony fingers trembling now and again as if in a troubled sleep. The sun poked a hole in the clouds, and for long moments I enjoyed the feel of its warmth. The lightest of breezes touched my face, and I flexed my nostrils, taking in the clean, cold air.

On my head I wore my knitted hat, and on that two bonnets I sewed into one, tied under my chin and held down by the stretched top of my shawl. It was all too much, too tight, too heavy, too close. I peeled them off and combed my fingers through my hair. It was flat and thin and oily, but the breeze felt nice on my scalp. I was tempted to rub sun-kissed snow on my bare head, but did not dare, so little do I trust the fickle weather here.

Still, we must take such moments when they come. Though I wish to God I had turned back after enjoying that hillside in the sun. But I did not.

Heartened and refreshed by sun, I walked on, keeping my hats in my hand a few minutes more. The only encumbrance was the shotgun. I did not continue climbing, but cut across the slope's face, heading westerly. One more ravine, I thought. What harm would it do to see what lay down there?

High up in a tall aspen a bird bounced on a branch. He was striking to look upon, with a long, twitchy tail, a black body, a white breast, and blue along his wings. He rattled out a string of calls, too many for one middle-size bird. The leaves that were left on the tree wagged and fluttered. Then he flapped off and I saw two more of the same birds arrow up out of the far side of the same stand of trees.

I must have startled them, I recall thinking. I slid down a patch of scree that snow had trouble staying put on, let alone a fifteen-year-old girl. At the bottom, I saw what had really startled the birds, and what I had, in turn, startled.

A large, sooty-colored wolf stood not forty feet from me. It was stone still, eyes wide, ears perked toward me, and head bent to one side as if confused.

I reckon it had been loping along what looked to be a well-used trail, narrow but packed by the comings and goings of many wolf feet. It was headed northward, and the trail curved beyond the wolf upward into a ravine I had not yet seen.

The wolf did not run, nor even startle. We stared at each other's eyes. My breath, unlike the wolf's, caught in my throat as if barbed. The corners of the wolf's mouth raised a little, as if it now understood what it was seeing and found it amusing. I saw the tip of its pink tongue moving slightly at the end of that long, parted mouth. Those eyes, brown ringed with gold at the center, never left my face.

Still holding my breath, I moved my left foot backwards, up-slope. Nothing changed. I moved my right foot, two fist-size rocks slid then stopped, held by the thin snow. I used the butt of the shotgun for balance. I had been carrying it by the tip of the barrels, an unwise thing to do, but not the dumbest I have done, as you will see.

I know not how long I stood poised, reliant on the feeble balance the gun gave me, my feet awkward on the graveled slope. My eyes were unable to move from the gaze of the grinning wolf, though I willed them to look away. Then I sensed movement to my right. North of the wolf, toward where it was headed, something moved. Several somethings. I pulled my eyes from his, finally, and wished I had not.

Wolves appeared as if conjured, melting into my view where moments before there had been only tree trunks and snow and jutting gray and black knobs of rock. The creatures looked ribby but strong, and all grinned at me from under wide, wet eyes. As with the first, their pink tongue tips pulsed with every slow breath.

Two among them were nearly black, others wore spattered gray coats, with thicker, longer hair along their backs and around their necks and heads. They numbered close to two dozen. I wondered how many more might emerge.

I have felt fear before this, as I have told this journal. I have felt it over and over again. But knowing I was the one thing all those wolves looked at jellied my guts and stopped my thudding heart. Then the wolves slowly spread apart, as if they were not moving their feet, so easily did they move, so quietly.

By the time my heart pounded once more, harder than it ever

has, the wolves had nearly formed a crescent around me. I was upslope of them, the closest still the first I saw. None took their eyes from me as they stepped, slow and confident, toward me.

I heard no birds, only the huffs of deep, chesty breaths from the wolves. What could I do but retreat back the way I had come? I was far from camp, too far. And I was a fool. As if to prove the point, I stepped back once, twice, and tripped, falling to my backside.

I jammed my heels into the hillside, sliding rock and gravel over the churned snow. Using the shotgun as a staff I pushed upright and the cold steel of the barrels felt safe and solid. I hefted the gun before me, still stepping backward, though slower and with care. I glanced back over a shoulder once, there were no other wolves behind me. I saw nothing but my own trail through the rock-knobbed snow.

Though I turned away but a moment, by the time I looked back the wolves had advanced and spread out more. They had the advantage over me as this was their home, their hunting ground. I felt certain they were the same ones who had tormented me at the nest.

I kept walking backward, and tried to think of any advantages I might have. My long skinning knife hung in its sheath on my belt, strapped about my middle, on the outside of my many layers of clothes. Good. I had already taken off the woolen socks I use as mittens. I jammed a hand into my coat pocket for the two shotgun shells I brought with me. Only then did I realize I still held my hat and bonnets. I thrust them under my coat, above the top button at my throat.

I walked backward faster, grabbing one shell at a time, my dirt-grimed fingers shaking. It was only then I noticed I had not done a particularly good job of washing my hands that morning. I mustn't let that happen, I remember thinking. Funny the things a person will think at such odd times. I gritted my teeth and forced my breaths to come out even.

The first shell slid into the barrel. Before I loaded the second, far to my left and downslope, I saw a wolf break into a run. Another did the same. The second was black and mangy, its hindquarters bony, and rather than run, it sort of hopped.

They were heading me off. I had to move faster, as they were surrounding me while I fumbled and stumbled on the slope. I had not traveled far at all from where I first saw the wolf. No time for the second shell. I snapped the barrel shut, thumbed back on the hammer all the way.

I sidestepped back the way I came, slamming into a knee-height boulder. I stepped around it and brought the shotgun up, jammed the butt into my shoulder, swinging it in a wide arc. This did not do a thing to slow the wolves. The first wolf followed me up the slope. I considered shooting at him, but he was still far away, and I was such a poor shot I thought I might miss. If the gun knocked me to the ground, which has happened before, then they would be on me.

All the while I swung the barrel left, then right. I broke into a lope, sort of sideways, trying to keep an eye on the advancing wolves. Those behind me kept a measured distance between us, their feet stepping sure, the muscles flexing beneath their hair, their grinning gazes never leaving my face.

I made short, whimpering sounds as I ran, stretching my legs as far as I could with each lunge. Soon I gave up trying to keep an eye on those behind me. I bolted full-out across the slope, jumped two boulders in my way, barking my shin on the second. I failed to see wolves upslope of me, nor any below, down in the trees. But I knew they were there.

I did not want to see that black one again, with its skinny, skulking body. That creature stayed fixed in my mind as I ran. I heard only my own boots stomping and crunching the snow and gravel, and then I was down at the base of the slope, in deeper snow again. Curse my stupidity. The wolves lunged at me, faster now, spread in a ragged line behind me. I squinted at the snow before me and made for my footsteps from earlier.

My skirts bunched and balled atop the snow, slowing me. I snatched them up with my free left hand and jammed a wad of hems between my teeth. I wore Thomas's trousers beneath them. Not for the last time did I think how unfair dresses are, though I wear them over everything else for extra warmth. Right then was no time to wax thoughtful.

Fifty feet to my right one, two, three low shapes lunged out of the tree line. The scant sun had softened the crust of snow in the open enough that the wolves broke through to their chests as they angled to arc wide ahead of me. But their misfortune was also some of my own, though I was able to maintain a decent pace as my legs are longer.

I tried not to think of the distance I still had to travel back to camp, or if I would be able to outrun them. All I had to do was keep ahead of them. My too-frequent glances over my shoulder told me I was not doing well. Wolves are powerful and used to such exertion in the snow. I am not.

I heard other breaths than mine, breaths that sounded measured and closer. Out of the sides of my eyes, dark shapes advanced. I was so close to the edge of the clearing, and then I would be into the trees where the wind had pushed the snow into stiff drifts, leaving stretches of lesser snow where I might gain time. But so would they.

I made it to the trees and looked back only once. That raggedy line of wolves still lunged in the snow of the clearing. Others, somewhere to my right, had likely angled back into the trees to get at me. My lungs were afire, but I concentrated all my thoughts on getting home to my nest. And so I did not see the tangle of root and rock as my right boot toe snagged beneath it.

I piled forward, whipping at the waist toward the ground, my head hit first, wrenching my legs, but my foot popped free. My right hand ripped from the shotgun. As my head smacked the frozen ground, I heard a tremendous explosion and my ears rang. I was up again in a moment, crawling like a baby, wobbling on my hands and knees.

My sight fuzzed, cleared, fuzzed, cleared again, and I heard screaming. No, that's not right, it was a yowling. I shook my head and pushed to my feet, my hand slapping at my belt for the knife handle. The fall had stolen precious time. I would at least face the inevitable attack.

But what I saw as I turned shocked me, and still does as I write this a day later. A wolf, perhaps the one I had first surprised, lay writhing on the snow a dozen yards behind, twisting and flipping, snapping its jaws. It was unable to run or do much of anything because its middle, behind the ribs, had been ripped apart. I did not understand right away. Beyond it the other wolves milled, sniffing and looking at me, then at the yowling wolf.

Perhaps they had attacked one of their own? I did not care. I ran, guessing I still had a mile to travel before reaching the camp. Soon, I told myself, I would be on my familiar trail, not that it would do me much good.

I glanced back and the wolves had split apart again. Some of them had set upon the bloody, writhing creature, and it looked as if they were eating it. Some of the others, maybe half of them, resumed their lunging efforts after me.

But they waited too long. When I dared another glance back, I saw only three of the wolves, the mangy black among them, still trailed me. The rest had turned back and were busy tearing into the other wolf and fighting amongst themselves. Eventually the three following me looked bored with the game and gave up the chase.

I did not let up. I ran as fast as I could. Even when the leather sole on my left boot loosened and began to flap, slapping like a tongue, front to back. It wasn't the best time for that to happen, but I stepped higher and did not slow down until I reached camp. I had almost made it to the edge of my little clearing when I risked another look backward. Nothing was following me.

That didn't slow me down one bit. I ran straight to the door of the nest, didn't bother to look around for signs that anything had tampered with it while I was away, and yanked hard. It popped free and I pushed my way inside. I shut it behind me and dragged the log across it. There was still daylight left but I did not care.

There was no way I was going to leave the nest again that day. Maybe not even the next, I thought. What if the wolves decided to follow me? What could an entire pack do? Surely they knew the route. Visions of their shiny eyes and grinning snouts, barely panting, tremble me anew each time I think of them.

Not until hours later, near dark, judging from the weak light angling down through gaps in the chimney hole, did I muster the courage to make a fire and think about food.

I made so many mistakes yesterday. I thought of the way the wolves moved soundlessly, with so little effort, jumping at me through the snow, catching up with me. I saw my boot catching, saw myself falling as if time had slowed down, saw the snow and rocks rising up to meet my face. Then that terrible booming explosion. What had that been?

And then I knew. It is absurd to me now that I did not think of the shotgun until that moment. I stood up from the bunk, panic gripping me. Even though I knew exactly where the shotgun was, I pillaged my nest, rummaging to no avail. The shotgun was where I had dropped it in the snow. And then another thought stopped me cold.

I shot the wolf that had been closest to me, the one who would have been on me when I tripped. Somehow, the notion sickened me, but not enough to throw me off my supper. I was hungry despite the day, or probably because of it.

I spent the rest of the night, as long as I was able to stay awake, stitching that flapping sole of my boot. I made it as good a job as I could, though I used up the last of Papa's waxed thread he had bought special for tack and canvas repairs. I used much of it already on various jobs that needed putting together.

It wasn't until I banked the stove and laid down that I noticed my hat and bonnets were not on my head. They must have slipped out of my coat when I ran. So careless of me. The day had rattled me, for I am not one to forget nor lose things. Now here in one day I lost what might be my most valuable possession, the shotgun, and I lost my hats. I had one other stocking cap and ways to mend up still more, but that is not the point.

I lay in bed knowing but not wanting to think about what I had to do the next day. I cried myself into sleep. It has been a long while since I've done that.

The day was made worse because I had been having a nice time, enjoying my walk in the countryside. But that is the way of things here. This life is feast or famine.

January ?, 1850

This morning, I talked to myself while I made breakfast, which wasn't more than a bite of meat I'd saved from my meal last night. I try to leave a mouthful or two from the previous day's food, plus I have a cup of tea of a morning. I'd long since drunk through all the coffee. That was a sad thing to have to give up, and soon enough my tea rations would wither, too. Despite that I have been using the same leaves for nigh on a week. It is the memory of tea I recall when I drink the hot water with limp leaves floating in it.

I told myself how foolish I had been the day before. Then I strapped on my knife, and forced open the door of the nest. It was bright, had been for a couple of hours. I breathed deep and headed out. I don't want to give the idea that I was doing anything brave. I took every step back along my trail as if it was a bitty piece of chocolate worth savoring, slow, slow, slow.

I hoped to find the gun and my hat and bonnets. But if the hats weren't near the gun, I decided I ought not go beyond that point. I figured I'd know where it all was, by the blood on the snow.

As I walked closer to the spot, I slowed my pace, and pretty soon I slipped that knife out of the sheath and waved it like I expected to be ambushed by cutthroats at a strange, foreign seaport.

I was breathing hard when I finally stepped from the trees. The flat ahead was mostly open and level, enough that I saw a dark spot. It had to be the dead wolf. I swallowed, looked left and right, and was about to step forward when I heard a scratching behind me. I spun, stifling a scream down to a whimper.

Watching me from atop a lump in the snow—a rock, maybe— sat a long-eared rabbit, his coat mostly white with gray-brown along the edges. One ear twitched, and its nose worked the air.

I let out a stuttery sort of breath, turned, and walked forward, careful to watch ahead and to my sides for any movement. But I saw none, not even curious rabbits. Soon I found the shotgun, triggers skyward, as it had fallen from me, its barrels pointed toward that dark spatter and smear on the snow less than fifteen feet behind where I'd fallen. I did not know it had been that close to me.

I grabbed up the shotgun, brushed away snow, and dragged a sleeve along it, as if that would help any damage that had been done by it lying out there all night. And that's when I saw the left-side hammer. It looked bent. I tested it, and it was indeed bent. And what's more, something looked to be missing. I held it close and squinted at it. Yep, something had snapped off. I knelt, pawing away snow gently, looking for something, but what I do not know.

I glanced up often, like a bird will do while it eats. Always on the lookout for a threat.

This entire occurrence with the wolves is one more thing that sets me up as the biggest fool that ever drew a breath.

February ?, 1850

I saw a pretty fox yesterday morning. I knew it was morning because my stomach was still growling like a baby bear hungry for a mouthful of anything at all. I have taken to eating no breakfast, a pinch of food at midday, then a little more along about sundown. I lessened my meals, as my greatest fear is to run out of food.

I do not believe I will be much of a hand at snaring rabbits, and I have not nearly enough shotgun shells to kill game of any size. That does not mean I don't still try to hunt. I attempted to make a bow and arrows, and while I managed something that worked, I lost two of my three arrows in the snow. One loss I can understand, accept it as the lack of skill of a beginner at something. But two is stupidity on my part.

I poked around in the snow, scuffing up a sizable patch, but the snow is deep, and in places the land slopes. For all I know those arrows are a good five, six feet down. After too much time spent rooting for them like a pig after acorns, I was out of breath, tired and shaking. I must learn to go about my days at a slower pace, lest I burn up the scant amount of food I take in to survive.

Cages as traps, that is another thing I have tried. I spent a good long while building a pair of traps big enough, or so I thought, to catch rabbits. I used a length of rope, unraveled it to make thinner ropes, and built a fine mess of woven branches and hairy little strings poking out here and there. I tried a second cage, made a better job of that, then rebuilt the first.

The next morning, I took them out along a well-traveled rabbit trail. But after a week, I caught nothing. There was not even sign of tracks nearby. I determined that rabbits are far too cunning for me. I am still puzzling it out, but maybe cages will work in the spring. Perhaps I'll use them up in the trees for other critters.

I have decided to try my hand at setting snares again, this time along that same rabbit run. At least I was a little familiar with how to make them, as William had been interested in such things a couple of years back. I helped him a time or two, but finally left him to it when he plain didn't talk while we were out along the creek. I got the feeling he wanted to be alone.

He is an odd duck sometimes. I find it difficult to figure out what is in his head. Then I reasoned that there is only room for me in my head, so why should he be any different?

In truth, I did not mind not going along, as every time I saw those poor bunnies hanging by their necks or their legs, and they caught sight of us coming along the trail, they set up a fuss, well, the ones that were still alive.

They set to twisting and screeching and squealing out sounds like a tiny baby might make, only worse. It didn't bother Will. Curious, though, that I don't mind the last bit, skinning and cutting them up for the stewpot. It's the killing I do not care for.

That said, I believe I am done being that girl. I could use some fresh rabbit. And if the smells attract bears or wolves or lions, so be it. I will fight them to the death over a fine pot of rabbit stew.

Now I need to catch a rabbit.

February, 1850

I mentioned some days ago that I wanted to catch a rabbit. Writing about my intention set me to thinking about how I might improve my skills. I'll be jiggered, as Papa says, if I am about to let bad luck or ignorance of a thing stop me from getting what I want.

I rerigged the snares, doing my best to mimic those Will had made. I tested it on my own hand so many times, I broke the snare. I used green whips. Well, being wintertime they weren't so much green as they were thin and young. The sap had all but left them. Still, they were more pliable than branches off full-grown trees.

I used forked sticks arranged to hold the snare hoop of twine low on the snow. I sprinkled snow along the twine to disguise it, then built up a small mound of what I hoped were toothsome treats to a rabbit—I soaked two dried currants in water to puff them up again. With my knife I whittled away the bark of a young branch to get at the green beneath.

I peeled off a dozen or so curls to resemble little shoots of green grass. They smelled good, too, reminded me of springtime and nice weather. I closed my eyes and sniffed them before arranging them in the middle of the noose part of the snare. I hate calling it that, but that is what it is.

I wished I had more than that to offer a hungry rabbit, but again, that is all there is. No matter how vicious the animals are hereabouts, I don't imagine there's a rabbit in these hills that would want a few thin slices of salty green beefsteak.

Once I had it all arranged to my satisfaction, I backed away carefully. I had two different snares kick off while I was still there. I took that to mean they were set too sensitive, but even if this one was, I'd rather not know until I am out of sight of the thing.

I am not going to starve yet without rabbit in my stewpot, but I am so tired of rank, half-rotted beef with a crust of salt (no matter how much I scrub it off with a rag and snow it is still salty), that in my mind I have developed a deep taste for rabbit.

A frigid spell was fast creeping in, so the rest of the day I spent doing the same thing I spend every waking hour doing— fetching firewood. And with each day it is a more onerous task, as my trail must be stomped anew with each snowfall. And there are fewer close-by trees all the time. I have laid low all the dry, dead standing trees within easy reach of the campsite.

I have chopped a number of green trees, but they are good for little. The flames on them tend to be low, bluish affairs that do little more than annoy me, throw scant heat, and hiss and pop like arthritic barn cats. I used some green logs as poles for the nest, and for their green boughs outside and in. I tried to do like Papa said of the Indians, and waste no part of a thing, be it a green tree, a dead tree, or the various articles of clothing I have made from one purpose into another.

I feel badly about Bub. If I had more time I could have done something useful with his hide, and on looking back I should have worked faster, saved the organs for eating, and picked clean each and every bone for the marrow. They would have made a sustaining soup.

An hour before dark I hauled a last armload of twigs and ratty branches back to the pile outside the nest. I stopped partway up my climb to my door in the side of the snowy mound, my footholds muddy hollows in the side.

I stared down at my left foot. It was a rag-wrapped boot that more resembled a head of swamp grass than a foot. What have I become? I thought. Not only am I tired and sore and hungry, but I am doing nothing but trudging through the routine of my days. And for what? I promised myself I would not think of the future, but instead make each day a thing to be wished through. But moments such as this will catch me by the throat and I find I cannot endure another minute of my life here in the snowed-in mountains.

February, 1850

It has turned desperately cold and my cursed fire will not throw heat. The wood sputters and hisses like a toothless old snake. Can't feel my fingers and the ink froze for good. I am carving the nib into the paper. I had hoped to use the last of it, then back to my pencils, but as with everything, the decision is not mine. Nothing to say. More tomorrow if I can get the fire to do more than smoke and hiss.

FEBRUARY, 1850

I do not want to be this person I have become. I remind myself of Widow Needlemeyer, who Papa spoke of as if she were the saddest thing he'd ever come across. Her husband had died so many years ago no one could recall much of what he looked like. About all they could agree on was that he did really exist. Beyond that he was a mystical character. But Widow Needlemeyer, she was a real corker.

I never said much to Papa about her, but when parents were around she was always kind as a cool swim on a hot July day. But when we were sent to help her with some chore or other— and it was usually me because I was the girl—why, she was a pinch-faced old thing with flint-rock eyes and a lipless cut for a mouth. Nothing came out of her mouth but sour-apple meanness. I do not know of any child who liked her.

My windy point is not that I wanted to recall that old woman at all, but at some time early in her life a bad thing must have happened that changed her. After that she nurtured routine, did the same thing the same way at the same time, day after day, all her life. As far as I know she is still doing that today.

And she is who comes to mind when I see myself in my routine. It is nothing I enjoy, but it is a way to fill the time each day. I wonder if that is the best way to be? What is so wrong with going inside the nest for the night and making tea and rereading passages from the Bible and Papa's travel guides, the same pages I have read hundreds or a thousand times already?

But I know that such a life is as deadening to the Janette deep in me as a wolf attacking me is to the outside of me. So I climbed back down, and watched my breath rise up in front of my face for a few moments. The day was a gray one and did not brighten as the hours lengthened.

Then I thought of the snare—I had forgotten it—and a smile came to me.

It was like a present sent by a mysterious person. There could be anything awaiting me. I reckoned there was still the better part of an hour of light left to me. So I set off with a kick in my step that hasn't been there in weeks. Anticipation drove me forward.

But nothing could prepare me for what I found.

I followed the short trail I had made leading southeastward from the camp. Within two minutes it brought me to the game trail that cuts across my trail. I follow along it, though not on it, for fear of leaving tracks that will scare off rabbits.

I try to be silent in the woods but it is of little use. I am not a graceful person at the best of times, and with my rag-wrapped boots the size of tree stumps, a rabbit would be hard-pressed to miss my sign.

I recognized the birches flanking the trail. The snare lay ahead, beyond a dip in the path. I heard a commotion, and seconds later I saw what made it. And it sickened me to my heart. It makes me feel the same way now, as I write this.

I had caught a rabbit in my snare, to be sure. But it was not even half grown. A baby, and it struggled. Even from my distance of twenty feet I could tell what had happened. Since it was so small, the snare had grabbed too much of the rabbit. The leg and shoulder had prevented the snare from snapping its neck.

It had broken its shoulder instead. I knew this because bone jutted through its storm-cloud fur. All around the wound a clot of fresh blood matted the fur and strung, freezing, to the ground. Each time the rabbit twisted and thrashed, more blood pumped out.

I must have made a sound, some exclamation, for the rabbit kicked with fury, squealing and spinning and twisting on the twine snare suspended by the bouncing, springing stick. I froze for the moment, not knowing what to do.

The most awful thing about the scene was the fear in the little rabbit's wide, unblinking eyes. Its mouth, with glinting teeth, stretched in a leer, and it made those high-pitched squealing sounds.

I hated myself at that moment more than I have ever hated anything or anyone. How could I ever do such a thing to another creature? One so innocent.

I thought perhaps that writing it down in the journal might help me be shed of it, might learn how to make it better. But then I think of that rabbit's eyes and hear its sad sounds, and I know I will be a long time in getting over it.

Papa and the boys would laugh at me, tell me I am being silly and sentimental. That the rabbit was put there by God for us to eat. And there is truth in that. If I had caught a full-grown rabbit, I would have felt bad. But I would have made a stew and done my best to tan the skin. That baby rabbit, though, cannot compare. It made me feel lonely.

You may tell by now that I did not skin that rabbit nor eat it. I slid out my knife, grasped the end of the blade in my socked hand, and whispered, "I am so very sorry." I closed my eyes and swung the handle like a short club. I delivered a blunt, hard blow to the rabbit's head, felt it hit, and I opened my eyes as the little back legs drew upward to the body, then sagged downward in death. I untied the snare twine, held the little body aloft at knee height, where it spun slowly while I decided what to do.

Then I did the only thing I felt would be appropriate. I kicked a hole in the snow to one side of the tiny trail, and laid the rabbit in it. It has been a long time since I held another living creature and the little rabbit did not change that. I had killed it and I suddenly felt weary and guilty and too weak to cry. I covered the little body with snow and looked down at it.

"Lord, please . . . let this rabbit into the Hereafter, and please forgive me for what I have done. I was greedy for stew." And do you know? Even when I said that little prayer, when I spoke that word "stew," I ran my tongue over my lips like an animal that can't help being hungry. But unlike an animal, I did not eat that rabbit. I wasted it. I killed it and I wasted it. Not like an Indian at all.

I take small solace in the fact that in this mountain wilderness, something, likely a fox or coyote or wolf or weasel, will find it and eat of it. But it won't be a Janette.

As I pulled down the snare, I knew it would be a long time before I felt comfortable in setting one again. Still, I reckon it will happen, especially considering how my meat supply is diminishing each day. I also learned that any dreams I may have had of a pair of luxurious rabbit-fur-lined mittens were gone. Good riddance. For now.

February, 1850

The fire died hours ago, must have been, because it's that cold in here. I can't see a thing, not that it bothers me. But I daren't light anything more than the nub of candle I am using to write this by. I suppose I am being silly and should light the fire, but I might run out of wood before daylight and I don't dare to open the door to fetch more.

You see, there is something out there tonight. Well, there is something out there most every night. But this time, on this night, something I have never heard before has walked in circles around and around my nest. I curse the snow for piling so deep. It helps keep the walls warm, of course, but it lets the beasts walk right outside the walls, right close to my head. Some of the smaller critters walk up and over the roof. But this is different. This one tried to claw its way through the roof. And it did not sound like a small critter. It knocked snow through the chimney hole, and bits of bark and branches dropped down on me.

Much more of that and the beast will fall through on top of me. I cannot imagine such a scene—me and a hungry, wild animal circling in this tiny space.

I should have added more braces when I built it, but I did not know the snow would be so deep. I also did not know there would be so many damnable animals. Nights are the worst time, because not only am I blind to everything out there, but that is when most of these creatures come out. And they are all hungry, which I cannot fault them for. But I do not want to be their meal.

I believe tonight's visitor is a lion. I don't have full proof, because though I have seen one, I had not yet heard one. We saw one not a week before we arrived here back in September.

It watched us from high up on a brown, rocky ledge well back, but overlooking the roadway. It was a long way off, and I had to hold a hand over my eyes and squint to see it at all. It was William who spied it first. He has exceptional eyesight.

At any rate, we paused the team and looked up at the rocks. Evidently Papa felt safe from the beast at that distance. It lay in a stretch of afternoon sun, baking and staring down at us with what looked to me like lazy eyes. It must not have been long since it had eaten as it showed no interest in us. It even twitched and curled its long tail as if it had nothing better to do.

Thomas snatched up a rock.

"Here now," said Papa, his eyebrows pulled together. "What is it you think you're going to do with that?"

"I aim to throw it at that big ol' cat. I want to see it jump."

"Oh no you don't." Papa wagged a finger in Thomas's face. "That is a wild animal, boy, and we don't know what it might get up to next. They are not to be trusted. I don't care if it's a squirrel or an elephant, I'll have no Riker go about riling wild beasts for no good reason."

Thomas dropped the rock. None of our commotion bothered that big cat. He sat up there, twitching that tail and ignoring us. And that is my only experience ever with a lion. Until tonight.

I am certain that's what has been stalking around outside. I am still shaking so I can hardly write this.

I spent the first few minutes after it woke me up lying as still as can be in my little bunk. I was so wrapped in quilts and clothes I did not know what to do, did not know what it might be.

It was still far off, and then it screamed again, closing in toward me. I say it screamed because it sounded like an angry woman's voice, if the sound had been dragged through hot coals. Oh, but it was a raw sound. The sound of something that did not care if anything else heard it.

And then it was upon me, right outside. It growled the whole time it was out there, husky and low, like thunder from a fast-moving storm, menacing and powerful. Sometimes it would grow faint, as if it might be leaving, only to start up all over again, inches away from me, and I knew it hadn't gone anywhere.

The snow was packed tight all around the outside of the nest. I suspect I should have built elsewhere, though where I do not know. Such thoughts won't help me on this night. Almost as soon as it came upon the nest, it set up that low growling, like a barrel full of river rocks tumbling, down deep, from the bottom of its gut.

It circled and circled. I pictured it, long black-tipped tail twitching, big feet and muscles working under a tight hide, on a lean, hungry body. I fancy I could smell it, too, and it wasn't at all like any stink I'd ever come across. It was a musk, dry and sharp, like death and life warring all at once.

I hadn't dared make a sound whilst it was out there, but I roused out of my fear stupor when I suspected it finally went away. I sat up, laid the shotgun across my lap and strapped the two knives to my waist. For good measure I pulled the two axes close by the bunk.

I sat on my bed, my back to the thickest wall. It was the sensible thing to do if the thing did what I would do if I were a hungry lion—try to dig me out. I reasoned I might gain a few more seconds by being close by the thickest wall. I should have known better.

February, 1850

The lion came back last night. I won't write much about it today, or perhaps I will, knowing me, but likely never again, because it is the closest I have yet come to dying. It happened again deep in the night when I was asleep. The fire was out, and I was doing my best to stay snug. The infernal wet has left me weak and with a constant shiver. I have to keep moving my arms and legs, sort of working them in circles and stretching them, massaging them with my hands because they pain me something fierce.

I had finally fallen asleep after I'd dealt with my aching hands and feet, when something pushed me hard on the back. I was asleep on my side, and it nearly knocked me to the floor.

Imagine in the dark, as dark as dark can be—not even moonlight or star shine can break into my little nest—something that shouldn't be there breaks in and touches you. In the small space you have carved for yourself, something knocks into you hard enough to wake you up. I can tell you this is not a good feeling. I had heard no noise to let me know what was coming.

Maybe I was sleeping soundly after being awake for so long with the aching, but I was more awake in that moment than I have ever been. I was so wrapped in nearly all our quilts and clothes, before I could sit up and swing my feet down off the low bunk I'd made, whatever it was raked me along my back. I yelped and shouldn't have, I know, but it was not something I could keep from doing.

It had dug down through the packed snow and clods of earth and canvas and lashed through my meager wall. It knew right where I was. And dark or no, I saw an arm of some sort, ripping and clawing at the air. It appeared long enough to reach across half the space of my little nest.

I rolled from the bunk, slammed into the little stove hard enough to knock the pipe loose. Then I heard it, the same as the night before, only closer and more frightening. A growl, long and loud, started high and dropped low and kept right on growling without taking a breath.

The shotgun, where was the shotgun? I wormed all over that little floor on my hands and knees, kicking at the quilts to get them off me, my hands shaking and me trying and not succeeding to keep from screams of my own. I scrambled in the sloppy mess that is my floor—half-frozen mud matted with dried and snapped pine boughs, clothes and bedding, a bit of canvas I had hoped would keep me from the mud.

My hands raked in the mud looking for the shotgun while that thing's arm sliced at the air above my bunk.

It lashed downward and grabbed a claw full of bedding, dragged it backward toward the hole, tried to force its way further in, as if it were being born in reverse somehow. But that is fanciful thinking as I write this and not what I was thinking at the time, I assure you. I cried out, shouting and sobbing, "No! No, no, no!"

All that did was make the thing more excited, and I saw more of that hairy leg and paw slashing through the hole. And the hole looked to be getting bigger with each second.

In the dark my hand slapped something solid, I felt along it— the shotgun—and dragged at it, pulling it closer to me. My hands shook so badly I felt certain I would drop the thing before I could pull back on the one hammer that still worked. I finally managed it and held the big gun tight to my shoulder, barely recalling the one meager shooting lesson Papa had given me so long ago.

I aimed above the bunk at the wall where I saw that arm grabbing air, knocking snow and bits of black things, what must have been my wall, slowly making the hole bigger. I saw the poles moving with the jerking and thrashing of the thing. Why I did not hear it when it had dug down for me, I also do not know. At that moment I did not care, I pulled the trigger and the shotgun clicked, nothing more.

I screamed loud, not so much out of fear, but in raw anger. "Papa, no, don't do this to me! No more, I can take no more!" I ranted, shouted oaths I am not sure are even words, but they are now. And all the while that beast lashed away, getting closer than ever to barging in on me.

I realized I was spending more time cursing the gun and fumbling and pushing myself away on my backside than I was fixing the problem. I yanked on the hammer again and felt it click back once, twice. I held the gun up, aimed at that horrible lashing arm, now shoulder and chest. I closed my eyes and pulled back hard on the trigger.

My nest exploded into millions of pieces! At least that is how it felt to me. The sound of the shotgun, something I had not heard in a small, tight space, was terrible. It filled my head with the roar of a thousand waterfalls and brass bands.

Yet even above that packed-cotton-ticking feeling inside my head, even through the blue smoke and sputtering sparks and tiny flames of the wall and cloth from clothes I had jammed against the wall, even then I heard the roar of pain and deep-rooted squealing and squawking of that beast.

The arm, the hairy clawing brute arm, disappeared by the time the smoke cleared, but the sound had not. I saw another leg, maybe a back leg, as the thing twisted around in the small tunnel it had dug for itself.

It kicked another cascade of snow in on my bed, but by the time I thought of shooting again, it had gone. I might have killed it had I been able to shoot again. Would that have been wise? I do not know. It would certainly have been one less animal out to kill me, one less thing to be frightened of.

These mountains are filled with hungry animals, and I am one of them. Though not as hungry as some. I suppose my hunger should be for life, not only for food. Then again, food is life, is it not? Oh, this is all too much for my addled brain, and my head is still filled with fuzz, and it echoes with the blast of the shotgun.

I take heart in the warm thought that I, too, have teeth, and I fight back. Now at least one of the beasts of the night knows this.

FEBRUARY, 1850

I spent a lifetime of minutes waiting for dawn to come.

Thin blades of cold light finally sneaked through the raw wound the cat and I made in my wall. The light found me still leaning against the disrupted stove. I was near frozen through. Where I'd been sitting, heat from my backside melted the icy mud of the floor and I felt as if I were sitting in my own filth.

I was not, and God willing I never will be, that helpless. But I sat as such for too long a time, cold as sin and beyond shivering. I knew I had to stand, and right the stove to make a fire, but none of it mattered. My mind could not make my body do a thing. I forced a sound that came out not as a word, but an animal growl. Still I did not move. I am dying, I thought. This is how it feels to die from too much of something, too much cold, too much fright, too much sadness.

One thing told me I was alive, and that was my breathing. I heard it rasping in and out of my throat, saw my breath before my face in the still air of my little hovel. As I sat thinking and not thinking, breathing, I learned, truly learned, I am alone in the world, and that I can only rely on myself.

It is something I should have learned months ago, but until that morning after the lion attack, I believed deep in my heart that Papa and the boys would come along any minute. I was certain, as soon as I'd busied myself at some task, I would hear grass or snow crunching underfoot, and turn and see them. They would be weary but smiling, striding toward me from out of the trees.

But that possibility died months ago. The horrible truth I have always known is that I am alone and will die here, newly fifteen years of age, not to see sixteen. All that remains is for me, Janette Riker, to make up my mind as to how long I want to live. I reckon this means I have given up on hope. So be it.

What other thoughts should I have?

I sat in stiff mud, shotgun in my lap, my frozen fingers gripped so tight around it I dared not move them for fear they might snap off. My left, for I am left-handed and rely on that hand more than the other, was uncovered the entire night. But it did not feel any colder than the right, which still wore the wool sock I'd pulled on when I went to sleep. I'd ripped the sock off my left when looking for the gun in the dark.

It took some convincing, but I managed to tell myself I should not give up, at least for as long as I have food. Food means strength, and if my body has strength, my mind will have it. When I run out of food, I will have no choice about life and death. It is a simple matter, really.

Until then, the mind needs to be fed like the body. But the mind needs fancier things than food. It needs to read and smell the fresh air, and then think about the words it reads and the air it breathes, where they come from. It needs to see birds and hear their pretty songs. It needs so much I have not thought of.

In such a manner I convinced myself to move from my frozen spot. One twitch at a time, one movement of a toe, one fingertip. I moved my lips, then my jaw, was able to open and close it, and my eyes, too. I must have blinked them all along, but it felt as if I hadn't in years.

I went on and on in this manner, and after a goodly while I dragged myself up off the frozen floor. At one point I grew convinced the beast was still outside, waiting to claw his way back in at me. This helped me move faster.

I kept at it and managed to stand. I am certain I looked like an old person, my legs all shaky and my hands aching so that I had to let go of the shotgun. The problem came when I tried to uncurl my fingers from it. I set the fingertips against the edge of the cold stove and pushed down to open up my frozen claws. It hurt mightily, and I moaned out loud, but it did the trick.

As soon as the gun dropped to the floor, I held my hands up and breathed on them, wondering if I had ruined them forever. That would make quick work of all that fancy thinking I did earlier. As soon as the stinging needle feeling ran up and down my fingers I suspected I was not going to lose the use of them.

Finally I was able to climb out of the nest. And I was glad I did, for the sun was up high, and though it was a cold day, the light cut through well enough and it warmed me like no fire could.

There was little wind, so I built a fire up by the wagon, somewhere above where the old fire pit sleeps in the snow. There is so much snow hereabouts it doesn't matter what is under it.

It's odd to build a fire in deep snow because as it burns the heat sinks the fire down until it hits whatever is at the bottom. I climbed back into the nest and pulled out two sizable hunks of salted meat and the shotgun.

I feasted like I hadn't eaten in months. I ate every bit, gristle and all, licked my fingers, licked clean the sticks I'd stabbed it on to cook it. All the while I kept a sharp eye for any critters that might be attracted by my feast.

The smell of cooking meat does not attract a killing beast such as a wolf or mountain lion or bear near as much as a fresh kill. It's the blood, I reckon. The cooking replaces that death stink with some other smell, one that beasts other than humans don't care for.

At least that is my theory. I don't much care if it is agreed with by anyone else. It makes me feel better, so that's all there is to it. But it did not stop me from trying to look in all directions at once. You never know when an animal will come at you.

After I ate, I sat by the fire and lost all caution. I dozed, though for only a short time. I woke to a pretty blue sky, but with a worrying thought. I was sleeping away precious time when I should have been repairing my damaged shelter. I also needed to fix up the stove.

Food has a way of making the hard things in life more tolerable. I hemmed and hawed and sighed and did everything I could to avoid the job at hand. I was acting like Thomas. None of it helped. So I got the axe and used it to smack loose the last of the logs I'd worked so hard to drag to camp for my firewood stores before the weather turned on me again some days back.

I had more wood than I remembered, which was good, as I figured I'd need much of it to help plug the tunnel that foul cat dug. I managed to free up five logs, leaving me one.

I climbed down into the hole. That gave me a creeping feeling, not only because I was right down in there where the cat had been, but because the hole it made wasn't big enough for me to climb through into the nest if I got trapped from above. Also, it stank something awful. I thought I smelled something off earlier when I was still inside. But man alive, it was worse down in that hole.

I got to scratching around down there, trying to wedge one of the logs in the gap it made, then patch the hole in the tarp. The dirt clods I'd spent so much time on? That cat had hauled them on out of the way like they were a child's woodblocks.

The stink, I soon discovered, was where that thing had fouled itself. It was frozen, so I did my best to scoop it up, blood, urine, and mess, and tossed it high up out of the hole. I'd deal with it later. Then I climbed on out and pushed the logs back in the hole.

I felt a small amount of satisfaction by seeing all the blood in the snow from that horrible creature. Which means I did get a good lick in at least. I admit to being disappointed on not finding the cat dead, or at least a ragged, bloody part of it frozen in the snow. The trail it took on out of here, its tracks flecked with blood, is about where I thought it to be, back toward the high rocks northwest of here. I will be satisfied if it stays put in its cave and licks its wounds. I will do the same. I call a truce, you vicious cat.

I reckon I will spend the next couple of days fetching firewood. Some of the trees, especially the wide, rooty ends, will have to be sacrificed down in the hole to line the outside of my nest. I hope that will keep out any other beasts looking to unearth me. There is the chance it will only slow them down.

Later, near dark, I loosened all five or six layers of coats and shirts and dresses and reached back behind me. It had not ripped my shirts or dress top. My fingers are still numb, and have trouble doing my bidding, but I felt welts in the middle of my back, raised and angry. The cat's claws had not cut into my skin when it pushed me, but it had gotten to me. In more than one way.

That cat haunts my waking dreams. I close my eyes and I see that slashing arm, hear the screeching and growling of it.

I will not sleep close to the wall again. I will build up more protection between me and the wall. I will sleep closer to the stove. I mostly end up all but hugging that little thing anyway.

February, 1850

While I poked my back, feeling those welts, I also felt something else. My bones. The bumps of my backbone popping out like knots on a stick. My ribs are spaced so that I can drag my fingertips up and down them. My shoulder blades, I don't even like to think about how they feel. Like the wings of a bird plucked bare.

I have all but given up on stripping down over the washbasin of warmed water to bathe. Not only because it is cold as blazes, but because it makes me feel bad about myself. I always was strong, had plenty of muscle, had to deal with the boys. But now, all this wood chopping and hauling is a trial. And I cannot get ahead on sleep. I am tired all the time.

My body is a sad thing. I fear if I ever took my clothes completely off I would look like one of those spring birds that has fallen too soon from the nest. You find them once in a while, dead or nearly so, on the ground, a mother robin swooping and fretting and hopping mad on a limb not far away. But the bony little thing isn't going to make it, and you wonder if maybe that is nature's way of saying something.

I wonder, too often for my own good, if this is all a trick. If it is nature or God or whoever playing with me as if I am a curiosity before putting an end to me. I wonder.

FEBRUARY (PERHAPS), 1850

It took all of my strength to climb out from under the bedding this morning. I had little choice, as there was no more warmth to be found in it than out of it. I soon learned why: The smoke hole was plugged with snow. I cleared it with much effort.

The days are short, so I force myself out. It is good to go into the daylight and move my legs. I dare not bathe much more than my face and hands. It is that cold. And besides, I could not bear to see my body now, all bones. My hinges, as Papa calls his knees and elbows, hurt more each day. My teeth, the same. Some are loose and they bleed, and feel as if they are growing, or else the rest of me is shrinking.

Everything about me withers and bleeds. How much blood can a body hold? How much can it give up? The teeth and the hinges ache so they keep me awake. Even the thin pleasure of sleep is taken from me.

March (though I am unsure), 1850

I cut myself. It is far from the first time, but it is the deepest. I have the bleeding staunched finally, though this page has a few dribbles of blood on it. I smeared them off and they look brown now, like all the rest of the mud on everything else I touch. The cut hurts like the devil, but it is my own fault. I was in a rush, and now I must pay the piper, as Papa used to say.

I have struggled with keeping an edge on the axe. I honestly don't know why, except maybe I am weaker than I was. I find it difficult to swing the axe, too, but that is not how I came to cut myself. As I say, I am no stranger to little cuts and stings and scrapes. I am about as blemished as a body can be, I expect.

One bit of goodness in all this is that my homemade leather mittens have worked suitably well. I cut them out of the satchel Papa used for lugging tools. They have saved my hands a heap load of pain, I can tell you. They let me grab wood I've lopped without digging into my skin.

But as to the cut I delivered to myself: I was hacking on a log like I usually do, sort of with my heels on the ground and my boot toes wedged against it. The dead tree, more of a pole, really, with the bark all but flaked off, rattled with each swing. When a dry stick like that is old it tends to put up a fight. It makes chopping tricky because it sends the axe back up again, even when you have a solid, honed edge.

I was cutting on that springy old pole, doing what Papa called making big pieces of wood into smaller pieces of wood, also known as making firewood, and I knew I should have stopped to sharpen that blade. But I was nearly through with the pile I'd dragged out of the trees. I thought I could finish, then sharpen the axe once I was done, get it honed for tomorrow.

I drove down with a mighty last blow, and instead of it springing outward like it had been doing, it whipped to the side. I think it was a combination of me being tired and not holding it firmly enough, plus that blade was dulled like an old tooth.

The axe head skidded off the wood, popped askew, and caught me in the shin. I felt it dig right into the bone. Then it bounced off me and flopped to the side. I dropped the handle like it was a hot coal, and froze for a few seconds.

"Oh Lord, what have I done?" I whispered, then sat on a stump behind me. I kept that wounded leg stretched out straight, as though it didn't belong to me. It may sound strange, but up until this point, even with all the little cuts and small injuries I'd dealt myself so far, I had not thought about harming myself badly.

But when I finally did, all manner of horrible thoughts flooded into my mind. I was in no state to give them the time of day. I gritted my teeth and lifted my skirts—all three of them.

Beneath I was wearing a pair of William's trousers, all trussed up at the waist, then two pairs of long underwear, my own and one slightly larger pair that belonged to William, or maybe Thomas, I don't recall. They are bulky but I don't mind. You get used to anything when you want to keep warm. And I long ago gave up on what I looked like. There is no one here to impress.

There was a lot of blood. My leg felt odd, tight and tingling. I wondered if the axe hit something that leaks and won't stop. Some sort of vein. I sucked air through my teeth and fought to keep my mind from turning fuzzy around the edges, then going black. I don't do well on seeing lots of blood from a person. A dead animal does not have that effect on me.

I forced myself to stay alert and aware of what I was doing. The cloth had been pushed into the wound. I bit the inside of my cheek hard, drawing more blood. I hurt at both ends then, too much to pass out. A scoop of snow did not help all that much, it turned red in my hand.

I recalled when Papa went to help at a neighbor's farm a couple of years back. Mr. Hendershaw lost a thumb because he looped a line around it when he was plowing.

Old Jed, his mule, stumbled, the line went tight, and there was a popping sound. Mr. Hendershaw looked up, saw that thumb of his spin up in the air as if a giant had pinched it off.

The important thing I recall Papa saying was that Mr. Hendershaw learned some things about doctoring from a physician when he was in the militia. He knew enough to slow the blood flowing to that hand, that way he would bleed out slower.

Mr. Hendershaw told Papa he felt bad for the mule. I imagine poor Old Jed stood there, looking dumb and guilty.

"Just like him," said Papa, "to worry on how the mule felt."

As I recall, Papa said Mr. Hendershaw cut those leather lines, took one end between his teeth, wrapped the other a pile of times around his arm, above the elbow, and did his best to tie it off tight. Then he held his arm up high so the blood would have to work harder to get to the wound.

Serious as could be, Papa said, "You will never guess what Mr. Hendershaw did with that thumb."

"He ate it," said Thomas.

Papa shook his head as if he didn't know where that boy came from. "He stuffed it in his trouser pocket. When he remembered it later, he rinsed off the field soil, and put it in a salty brine. Then he sealed the top tight, and there it sits."

"No," I said.

Papa nodded. He knew what my next question would be. "I

reckon Mr. Hendershaw would show it to you if you ask kindly. And maybe brought him a loaf of your bread." He winked.

And that is what I did. The thumb looked more like a puckered garden grub than a thumb. But the important thing is that I remembered I had to slow down the awful bleeding my leg was doing. I clawed off the leather belt I had buckled around my middle, over my outer coat. Then I slid the two knife sheaths off, and wrapped that belt around my leg above the knee. I dragged on the end hard, then laid it back on itself and wrapped the rest, keeping it tight all the while.

When I had but six or so inches of the belt left, I jammed the end beneath the wraps. I hoped it was tight enough, because it ached something fierce. My leg from the knee down began to throb, but whether that was a good thing or a bad thing, I did not know. I also sat on the snow and raised my leg up, propping it on the stump, following Mr. Hendershaw's logic of making the blood work harder to get to the wound.

I wasted no time in inspecting the cut further, continuing to pack snow on it, then pull it away once it reddened with blood. I began to feel cold, colder than I usually felt. That was a sign of something bad, I felt certain.

I bit the inside of my mouth again, and my eyes teared with the pain of it. But I managed to clean the wound by drawing handfuls of snow over it. The blood welled out of the gash, though slower than before.

I didn't know what else I could do. Until the blood stopped, I was not able to go much of anywhere and I only had at best two hours before dark came.

I looked at the bloody snow and my heart flopped like a beached fish. What if all that blood smelled like something tasty to an animal? What if, what if, what if? I did my best to stop thinking of all those possibilities, worrying me to no end.

I ate clean snow and thought long and hard about what to do

next. The cold and wet snow helped clear my head. I got my breathing back down to where it should be. No sense getting all nerved up, girl, I told myself.

After a good hour, the bleeding stopped and the top of the cut looked to be stiffening like the skin on a gravy. I took that as a good sign. It hurt like hellfire, but I tightened the belt. My leg had stiffened like a log, throbbing and angry feeling. It was swollen in pretty good shape, too. I gritted my teeth and stood.

It took me a little while, and I remembered to toss my knives and axe down ahead of me so they landed in the snow below the door. The leg began to bleed again, and I felt it trickling down into my socks and boot. I tossed the firewood I'd gathered down toward the nest. If I was bad off tomorrow, I'd want wood close by. I reasoned my leg would need a couple of days to recuperate.

By the time I made it down there myself, skidding and sliding down the embankment, my leg was paining me something awful. But I had to keep on. My teeth were gritted so tight I thought they might crack. The worst was yet to come, and I don't mean lobbing wood through the door.

It took me a long, long while to hoist myself up through the door. By the time I made it to my bed, I was near passed out from exhaustion. But I had to take full advantage of the daylight still coming in through the doorway. My lamp oil had long since given out and candles would not be sufficient for what I had in mind.

I blew on coals in the stove, added tinder, and kindled a small fire. Then I rummaged and found my sewing basket. I'd last used it to mend holes in my mitten socks. I was forever mending something. But at that moment I had to mend my body.

I chose the cleanest thread I could find, then heated the needle quickly over a tiny flame. I sopped up the blood crust off the cut again, keeping my leg raised as I had earlier.

This time the leg didn't want to give up so easily. It bled and showed no sign of slowing. I yarned on that belt, working it even tighter, and my leg hurt worse than ever. But it eventually worked. I wasted no time, and stuck my needle in above the two-inch gash. It looked like one of those slits you make in the top of a pie crust before you bake it. Only imagine if the pie was a fresh raspberry, all that ooze bubbling under the crust waiting to leak through.

The needle slid through easier than I expected, and I drew it out again. I told myself it was no different than mending a tear on one of the boys' sleeves. I used the bottom of a clean blue shirt to dab the blood and help keep it clear enough for me to see what I was doing. That needle was difficult to grasp, but I made sure not to space my stitches too far apart lest it open again.

Somehow, as I sewed, the pain sort of stayed the same, not getting much worse, not letting up. That was as much of a gift as I was allowed, though.

As soon as I finished and tied it off, I flopped back down on my bunk intending only to regain my strength. I still had to close my door tight and draw the bar, then make sure the fire kept burning. It is a trial to light with the flint and steel.

But that is not what happened. I fell asleep and woke many hours later, cold. Cold to my bones. The door was open wide, as I saw stars through it. When I sat up my head dizzied, even in the dark, and it was an effort to right myself.

I think perhaps it is even worse in the dark, for there is nothing much for the eyes to focus on to help remedy the dizzy feeling. That is my amateur opinion, anyway.

My second thought was of my leg, and that it should be hurting worse than it did. I reached down gingerly and was shocked to find it had swelled up to four times the size it normally is. It was cold, colder than the flesh of a dead thing. I uttered cries of fear then, I don't mind saying.

I left that leather belt cinched too tight for too long. I grabbed at it, but my leg had swelled up around it as if it were somehow pumped with water or air. It didn't feel much like my leg, but felt like I was digging at some other person's limb.

I found the end I'd tucked in under the rest and worked with my fingertips, grunting and making little crying sounds that did not embarrass me one bit. I knew I had to get that belt off there lest I end up killing the entire leg. And if that happened, I was surely dead myself, for there was no way under God's blue sky I could saw off my own leg to save the rest of me. I would be like an animal in a trap without the will power to chew on through and leave that dead limb behind.

I had never been in such a desperate situation. My leg was a thick, fleshy log that did not feel a thing I was doing to it, even after I unwrapped the belt. I whimpered and howled and struck at it with my fists.

I decided after too many tears that it needed time, since the whole thing didn't get this big and horrible in a few minutes. Time tells all, as Papa said when he didn't quite know the answer to something. Then he'd lay a finger alongside his long nose and wink. I think he liked to pretend he was being clever, knowing all the while he was full of beans.

I also decided my poor leg needed heat. My nest is small enough I am able to lean out, rest an arm on a crate, and blow into the belly of the stove to revive coals. My hands and arms were shaking, though not from the cold but from weakness and fear. I thought of little else other than I had likely killed myself. I might be on my way to a painful, slow death in my nest. All because I cinched that leg too tight for too long.

March, 1850

There is little fun in my days. And when there is it is a small, sweet thing soon pinched out by worry.

Today I saw a chickadee, and watched him for long minutes, lost in the moment of sunlight and the small darting way he had of dancing from one thin branch to another, pecking at tiny bugs he found toothsome. Soon he flew close to me, landed within five feet of me and regarded me as something he was unsure of. I sat so very still, held my breath, kept my eyes from blinking, and do you know? He landed on me!

I did not feel him through my layers of wool and cotton clothing, but even if I wore a thin shirt that little bird was so light I might not have felt him. I shifted my eyes without moving my head, and saw him out of my left eye.

He stood near the end of my shoulder, pecked once at a seam with threads sticking up like caterpillar legs—likely what attracted him. He soon fluttered off as quickly as he landed. I wish he had stayed a little longer. That would have been grand with me. Not since hugging Bib and Bub have I been so close to a living thing that did not want to do me harm. (I do not count the rabbit, as it was in death agonies because of me.)

Since my leg is not yet healed, though greatly improved, I drag myself up and down the steps I have built inside in order to get to my little doorway. The steps consist of two small crates and one nail keg atop a small steamer trunk. I propped the trunk on a layer of rocks because it gets wet at the bottom when the stove heats up. It helped somewhat, but I have a devil of a time keeping my food, such as it is, dry.

I feel sickly much of the time and there is a rising stink coming off the salted meat. That happens every time we get these warm days. Such is the smell that in the midst of this warmth it is all I can do to reach in the bins and shuffle the meat to coat it again in what salt remains.

I was tempted to pack snow in with the meat, thinking the chill might help. But I thought it might wash off the salt instead. And if the warmth continues, the snow will melt anyway, and the meat will rot faster. At least with the salt on, I stand a chance of having some edible bites left.

I decided to cook whatever hunks look rank. I had to cut off a goodly portion that went green. Some of it was worse than I thought, and it made me cough and gag as I sliced it. My eyes watered, too, but I got the job done. I saved what salt I could, hoping that if it had touched the tainted meat it wouldn't carry the taint to the fresher meat. But I don't know. Time will tell.

As for the rest, I cooked up the questionable scraps and ate my fill, as I knew it would go bad soon anyhow. But that was only one meal, then I restrained myself from feasting.

It was a good thing I did, too, for the bad weather came back hard and fast, and with it the snow and gray skies.

Now I am in the midst of dreariness and cold and slicing wind. I don't know how much longer it will last, nor do I want to know. I am better off wondering each day if there is an end in sight.

If I am still alive come spring, I will have to walk on out of these mountains. Though with my game leg I am not at all certain I will be able to contend with the hardships I might face. I will not likely be able to outrun determined creatures. I do not write that with pity in mind, but as a matter of course.

MARCH, 1850

When I was younger, Mama said I had too fanciful a mind. That may be true, for I prayed that the sound that haunted me last night was nothing more than the wind. But no, my mind is not as clever as the thing I heard. As to what it was, I am unsure.

I do not think it was a bear. Papa told me bears sleep away their winters. It strikes me I am doing much the same, though in fits and starts. I spend much of my time sleeping, or as near to it as a body can get without being asleep. It is a lazy way to live, but there is little I can do about it.

I wonder if this is what a fool feels like, if old Clarence Bugbee from back home felt like this, trapped in his cracked mind, staring at the world around him as if he was newly born, or had never been awake before. Papa said he was fine until his father accidentally knocked him on the bean with the post maul. They had been setting fence when that mashed-wood head of the great mallet slammed down onto Clarence's own head. He was not but ten years old—

It is later, hours later. I had to leave off in the middle of that silly story about old crack-minded Clarence because the sound came back. Though I still do not know what it was, I can tell you it is not any animal I have ever heard.

MARCH, 1850

Should I die out here, all alone, it is far more likely that I will be eaten by animals, the very animals I have come to respect and loathe, all at once. I do not care if that makes sense. That is the way of things with me. My life has withered to two things, making fire and finding food. Everything else about it has become more complicated than anything I have ever done.

I do not want my body to be chewed on and fought over by animals, my bones to be dragged off to wolf dens and buried in dirt by grizzlies and gnawed on in rocky caves by lions. If I am to die I want to protect my body somehow. If I am wrong and Papa and the boys are still alive, and one day are able to make it back here, then they would know I waited for them. I have put so much work into waiting here, I must see it through.

March, 1850

As I mentioned some days ago, I have only two concerns—food and fire. Fire and food. And it is my fondest hope that once the weather becomes warmer I will be able to dispense with making fire—at least of a size big enough to warm me.

If I do not manage to kill food, I will not need fire for anything, for I will be dead. That is the beginning and end of it.

My last hope is that I will be found by a group of travelers who chose the same route as did we. I have tried to figure out the earliest someone might leave Missouri or anywhere east of here. Even if they were to depart now, it would be months before they made it to me, if they chose to travel this northerly trail. It does not appear likely.

It has become trying to concentrate on such concerns. I need more food, better food. I cannot wait for spring so I might feel warmth once again. There was respite from the cold some weeks ago. Warm winds surprised me when they blew over the mountains from the west.

I thought for a time, was convinced of it, actually, that winter was leaving me. It felt good, though too early. I was suspicious of it. Still, I came to believe, wanted to believe, that the great Rocky Mountains, for all their size, had suffered a less extreme winter than other places. The warm winds melted snow and the sun warmed my bones. I lay out in it, on my back atop the roof of the nest, well enough away from prowling creatures, should any dare approach. And I let the heat soak into me.

For many days it was lovely and perfect. Great patches of brown grasses peeked out as the snow sunk into the earth. Channels opened on the river, wider each morning. I allowed myself happiness. I smiled for the first time in weeks, months, who knows how long? But it did not last. I should have known nothing good ever lingers.

One afternoon warm air of a kindly Mother Nature breathed on me from the west. I watched the blue sky, speckled with white clouds far off and high, then dozed in the sun when I should have been gathering firewood. That was how convinced I'd become that the fine weather really was spring. Some time later a sudden cold breeze woke me and I gasped. I even sat upright before my eyes opened. The sky had turned the color of ash, blackening as I watched. That night, snow fell and the air chilled so that I wondered if the warmth had happened at all.

March ?, 1850

Two days ago, it appeared spring finally decided to grab hold and do its job. That abiding news came in the form of a whole lot of melting snow. My nest was a dripping, sagged thing that sunk into the earth more with each minute that passed.

I had tried for ages to clear the roof of snow, and while I did manage to shift a goodly amount, it still leaked like a slow rainy day inside the nest. Some better solution had to be found. Since I had grown tired of being wet and cold and forever dwelling in the dark, I resolved I would once more set up my camp back in the wagon.

It took some doing to get to it from my nest, as the mud close by the river grew deeper overnight. It was nearly to my knees. I tossed ahead of me on the path the rangiest branches left over from my recent efforts at shoring up the nest. They were ragged sticks useful for little more than stepping on. I still sunk into the muck, but found if I moved quickly I kept from disappearing. I could have lost a boot had I not stepped lively.

Still, by the time I made it to the wagon my skirts were black. It was cold enough that mud caked in frozen clumps that swung and knocked into my legs as I walked.

I made it to the nearest wheel. Thankfully I had taken the socks off my hands before I set out on my short but eventful ramble. I hoisted myself up and sat, leaning to one side because the seat is broken. For a few moments, the stiff breeze wound down to a tickle, and something warm and lovely touched my face like the gentlest of hot breaths. I looked up to see a thing I had not witnessed in what felt like weeks. The sun, unadorned by dark clouds!

Gray threads of the cuffs of Papa's woolen shirt danced on my grimy knuckles. I closed my eyes, my face bent upward. After a moment I smiled and pulled off my hat, then slid the rawhide thong out of my messy, stiff hair. I shook my head a little, not daring to tempt the devil who manages that wind.

I sat that way for a time, let my shoulders sag, felt the heat on my cheeks. I turned my face this way and that, not daring to open my eyes for fear that precious sun might turn tail.

It was then I heard a far-off sound, a cracking rumble to the west, from that narrow mountain cleft I had trekked so many times. I opened my eyes and looked upstream, quite sure I looked like Belle, our old hound, when I would ask her if she wanted to take a walk around the fields. She would tilt her head, her eyebrows rising together. So there I sat, performing my best confused dog pantomime.

The sound was still there, but louder. A thunderstorm? No, this was different. I decided to get back down to the nest where I'd have a better view upriver. I had given thought to hauling some of my goods back to the wagon anyway, as the nest had proven far too wet. The task would take a month of Sundays, but time was a thing I had in abundance.

I snugged my hat back on my head, and from inside my coat pocket I felt this very journal and pencil nub bump against me as I stood. I tugged it out—a corner caught on the pocket edge, snapped threads. I set it on the bench seat, then climbed down, splat into the muck. I tugged myself free, leaning on the wheel for support. The mud sucked at my rag-wrapped feet, but I freed them enough to climb onto my mess of branches. All the while the sound grew louder.

I slid down the path toward the nest, reached for the curve in the root I knew would be there, the same handhold I had used all winter, gone smooth with use, and swung myself around.

There was the river in a raggedy angle, still mostly silver-white and topped with ice and snow, though brown rocks had prodded through for days. That meant the ice was shrinking beneath.

As I watched, dank brown water seeped from beneath the ice up around the rocks. New cracks in the ice lengthened, widened, and filled with that brown ooze. I didn't have long to puzzle it over. I soon realized it wasn't the sound I had to worry about, it was the thing beneath it. It was the river.

Imagine a huge gate blocking the river, holding back more water than you ever thought you'd see at one time. Now imagine that gate lifting and that water bursting straight at you. That is what I saw.

My mind did its best to snap to attention, but it was like a weary soldier who has marched too long. The river, I thought. The river, of course it's the river, flooding, rising with the melting snow. I had built too low, too close to the river and now it was all going to be over in seconds.

Move, girl! I shouted at myself.

I clawed my way back up the muddy bank, and I nearly made it, too. But then my rag-wrapped foot caught on a root. I swear it poked right out of the mud like an old crone's hand, and snagged hold of me. There wasn't much I could do, as by then the water was on me. It slammed me, foot to head, and burst over me. I was upended, pulled away from anything solid, but not for long.

All manner of hard things poked and slammed into me, knocked me upside my head, tugged at my hair, whipped my arms in unnatural directions. I tried to scream but I was surrounded by muddy water that filled my nose and mouth and ears and eyes.

When I thought I'd reached the end of my luck, I was shoved into a run of fast-moving water that carried me with it and stopped me from being thrashed and pulled and pushed in every direction at once. It popped my head above the water long enough for me to see I was far downstream from where I had spent my winter.

I knew it because in that glimpse above the brown water I saw the top of the wagon ribs in the distance. Everything between me and it was a sea of brown water. I have never seen the ocean, but that's what it must look like. Water, everywhere.

I was dunked, then pushed up above the water again. So quiet below, yet so loud, like thunder, above. I spit water, gagged, and tried to breathe all at once. I reached to grab onto something, anything, and found myself shoved into the riverbank. Alders and spiky, mashed trees poked up in a sort of line that must have been the edge of the river. If I followed that to my right I might be able to get into shallower water.

To my left ran the channel where the river had been—still was—though now it was a killing thing. Everything around me stunk like muck and raw earth.

I was a sight, I am sure, coughing and retching as I grabbed for the wagging ends of a riverside tree, its top sticking out of the bubbling brown mess. Then I could move no closer—my left foot was stuck fast. I tugged and tugged, shifting my position in hopes of twisting my foot. Must have been roots. I faced downstream, and saw the white boil of floodwater far in the distance, still racing.

I could not believe the river I had known for so long, the frozen, quiet, low thing among the rocks, could be the same as this. I hoped animals drinking downstream had more wits about them than I did. Of course they would. Wild animals are smarter than any person could ever hope to be.

As I turned upstream, still working on freeing that foot in the bouncing, jumping root tangle beneath me, a tree came at me, bigger around than what I could circle with my arms.

It was a dozen feet from me, spinning slowly in the flow and fixing to slam me a good one. I had nothing to protect me, no way to save myself. In seconds it would hit me hard. So I did the only thing I could do. I gulped air fast and dunked myself under once more, this time choosing to do so. I prayed I was low enough for the log to pass over me.

It never occurred to me that the log would have horrendous branches under the water acting as rudders. But that's what it had. Long, raking claws drove into me. I felt something push and push into my breadbasket, as Papa called his chest, then something snapped. I wasn't sure if it was my chest caving in or the branch giving way.

It pushed me along with it, this time underwater. I was in a world of hurt. Water filled me again and I felt whatever little edge of light I had regained slipping away, fuzzing and numbing me. I hurt less and my arms and legs stopped thrashing.

Then the log must have rolled and spun away in a different direction. And like that I was up once more, bobbing head above water. Needless to say my foot was free, though it throbbed like a bag of stinging bees. I figured it was broken, but I didn't care. I was alive, and thankful to be freed of whatever roots had held me, trying to make me one of their own. I pictured a tangle of my bones snagged in roots, picked clean by fishes and whatever else was down there.

I thrashed and flailed and tried to recall how to swim. To my right, maybe fifty feet away but coming up fast, was a slope of grassy, snowy riverbank.

For every dragging stroke I made toward it I was pulled downstream another thirty feet or more. Still, I made for the bank. I decided I could not let the water win, not when I was so close.

Sooner than I expected, my feet touched something, bounced off, touched again. It was the bottom, and with each reach and pull I made through that rushing water, I felt more land beneath my feet. Soon I was touching the river bottom with each step.

And a good thing, too, as I could not last much longer. It was a race between me and the water. Would I make it to safety before my body gave out? As soon as I let that thought worm its way into my brain, I grew angry with myself, an emotion I am familiar with, having lived cheek by jowl with it for so long.

I collapsed sooner than I ought, but there was nothing for it. As played out as I was, and despite all my talk of feeling a strength inside me, I was willing to lie there and let the water, warm in the shallows, bubble up and around my face. I had been so wet of late, the feeling of more water sliding into my nose, plugging up my ears, and clamming into my eyes didn't much bother me any longer.

That would have been the end of me had the thing not touched me, nuzzled up to me like I was a mother and it was fixing to suckle.

I say "thing" because that is all I could think of at the time. In truth it was not an unpleasant feeling, this warm, weighted soft . . . thing. There's that word again, but that is what I thought as I lay face down in the water willing myself to give up and die.

But the thing kept touching me, bumping up against me as if to get my attention. I let go of the notion of dying, and with all the strength God has given me on this mortal world, I lifted my face from the water. Mud, ice, and muck creamed together, drizzled down my cheeks. I looked to my left side, for that's where the thing was.

I screamed.

Let me tell you, nothing revives a near-dead girl quicker than a scream. Especially one from her own self. With my arms behind me, I churned in the mud to get away from that soft, warm thing. Then I saw what it was . . . a freshly dead animal. Only I didn't know at the time it was dead. I saw a fanged snout, black lips pulled back over red-black gums, long curvy teeth, white, gone yellow at the root, one had snapped in half. The eye stared so like a person's, as if to tell me I'd best prepare myself because it was fixing to lay into me and peel flesh from bone.

But it didn't move. Not of its own strength, anyway. The unending push and slop of the water moved it. Finally I looked away, knowing it was dead.

Though the river was still a mighty snake of brown filth, pulsing and thrashing, I had been lucky enough in my unwitting way to have steered myself into a side channel. I am inclined to think it's called an oxbow. I may be incorrect.

A gust of wind and a rush of current nudged the dead thing into me once more. I admit I yelped again, and did my best to crawl from it. But this time I did not take my eyes off it. I saw it for what it was, the carcass of a dog of some sort, perhaps a wolf or coyote.

It looked to have died fighting, filled with anger and determination and a lack of fear. None of which I felt. I had, after all, been willing to let myself drown. Then along came that poor creature, nudging into me with its open-face snarl, staring me down.

I raised a toe to nudge it. The body spun slowly, bobbing, the muddy water edging up, puckering its fur and washing over its unblinking brown eye. As it floated free, bobbing near me, I saw it was not full grown. Likely it had been caught unaware, maybe snug in a den, then unearthed by water and thrashed beyond its will to live.

Wouldn't you know it? Tears like I had not felt in a month of forevers ran down my mud-packed face. I tried to wipe them but only succeeded in cramming more mud into my eyes. That stung and I cried some more because it all was so unfair, and the whole while the poor half-grown wolf lay in the shallows staring at me.

Pretty soon I decided I needed to do something, anything that was a boldness, a defiance toward that river, toward the mountains, toward this entire place.

I dragged myself off my backside and faced the river, as if I did not trust it—which I most certainly do not. I plunked down on snow and poking grasses. The dead critter stared at me. I stared back. Then I pushed myself to my feet, wobbly at first. I reckoned I took more of a knock-around than I first thought, but I waded back in the ten feet or so to the sodden mess of fur and teeth and grabbed it at the shoulder. The skin was still loose and its body limp. It had not been dead for long.

I dragged it up to the knob of high ground I had seen from the river, and laid it at the top. It was the sanest thing I could think of doing at the time. It was a dead beast, I know, and maybe its parents were my tormenters, but they did so because they had young. This one, maybe others.

All I could think of was how alike that little wolf and I were, both half-grown, both snug in our dens, both taken by surprise by something doing its best to kill us off. I was still sobbing, for the wolf and for me. I deserved it, and I reckon the wolf did, too.

I knelt by the young thing, even younger-looking out of the water, its dark coat matted with mud. I patted it a time or two more then pushed myself back upright, an old woman long before my time, and made my way slow as I'd ever moved back toward the only thing I had left in the world, that old wreck of a wagon. I hoped it was still there.

MARCH ?, 1850

March is for suckers, as Papa says. I heard him mutter that my entire life, whenever that month came up in the almanac. I never gave it much thought beyond the fact that he never looked happy when saying it. As I stared out through the cracked and sprung ribs of the wagon, past the flapping, ragged canvas I had dragged out of the swollen river. A cold wind bit at me like a starving rat. Yes, I finally knew what Papa meant about March.

I was looking at what he always looked at when he said it—a heavy, wet snowstorm. It pulled the pins right out from under me, a sucker for having fallen for the allure of spring.

As far as the jutting peaks in the distance, I saw nothing but a blue-white land. And it was all snow. Nearly to my knees. The river was even shrouded by it, puffed clumps as pretty in the sun as a confection I could only dream of baking. Yet, despite the deep heartache I felt at seeing all that cursed snow clinging to everything, I knew it could not last long. The calendar would not let it.

I played a little game and closed my eyes. I told myself when I opened them all that snow would have turned into pan-fried cornbread. As you may have guessed, I opened my silly eyes and wonder of wonders, it was all snow, not a crumb of cornbread in sight.

There is one good thing to have come from this morning's depressing view: If Papa is correct, that might mean it's March, though something in my mind nudges me into thinking it is closer to April. Does it really matter?

Days back, after my nest flooded, I had made my way upstream to the wagon. I was sore and tired, so it took longer than it might have, but I made it by nightfall. It was all I could do to climb into the wagon. Finding this diary on the seat, waiting for me like a friend, warmed me nicely. That was all that did, however. In a way I was glad it was near dark, so I wouldn't have to see what a wreck my nest had become. That night I curled up in the wagon and pretended I was not cold. It did not work so well.

The next morning, I watched the sun brighten the valley. The river had become a slow-moving brown thing three times as wide and deeper than it had been. I had no food, no way to make fire, no possessions to speak of, save for the wagon and the jumble of crates and few tools I'd left in it. There is a shovel, Papa's scythe handle, a broken wooden pail, short, frayed hanks of rope, a chain.

I was hungry, but that was not a new notion. Without any food at hand, even rotted meat, my weak feeling would soon become worse. I climbed down from the wagon once again and made my way to the river. The nest was mostly gone, though some of the ribs poked above the slow brown water. Might be my stove was under there, but it would do me little good. I wondered how long the river would stay high.

The valley is filled with snow, though it is melting, as told by the number of brown bumps of grass poking through, like heads of critters waking up. That said, there is a whole lot of snow still to melt. The mountains all around are mostly white, top to bottom, save where patches of pines and gray boulders show themselves.

Then all that snow will find its way to the lowest place. Papa always said water seeks the easy path. Then he would look at Thomas and say, "Don't be like water, son." Here, that would be the river. So any chance of finding my goods was gone for a time, or for good. Most of it likely washed far downstream. I didn't much care. Still don't.

My spirits perked as I walked along the bank. As I said, I found a ragged bit of the wagon cover, which had been the roof of the nest, snagged in alders that whipped my face, refusing to give it up. I dragged it back to the wagon and laid it across the ribs to dry in the sun. Might keep me warmer at night.

I went back to the river the next day and had nearly given up when I found two more of my things. Only two. One of them was a cotton sack I almost passed by, so black was it with mud. Its drawstring had tangled in the roots of a washed-up tree. I untied it and found two or three handfuls of wet cornmeal. I am quite certain I made all manner of animal sounds as I ate that foul paste. I forced myself to eat but half of it, knowing the rest would have to last me. It tasted of river and mud, and not at all of cornmeal, but I knew what it had once been and that was enough.

The second and last of my possessions I ever found was my most favorite, and the one thing in all this long winter that made me feel good inside. You might think it was the cornmeal that would do that. But no, this was a piece of the last of Mama's china teacups. That one I had been saving. Now there isn't enough left of it to be useful in any way except to look at. The little loop of a handle and a wedge of cup, that's all.

I found it hanging, neat as you please, a few inches above the water on a stub of branch that bobbed in the slow current. The pretty painted blue flowers caught my eye. I nearly slipped into the water retrieving it, but I didn't care. It means the world to me and I hold it gently in my filthy hands and look at it whenever I am not writing in this diary. I am holding it now.

I even sniff it, as if I can smell the flowers. No, not the flowers so much as the kitchen back in Missouri. I close my eyes and there we all are, Mama and Papa and William and Thomas. I smell wood smoke and cinnamon and a bubbling stew and the warmth of fresh bread and the little bit of burned smell of Papa's coffee simmering on the back of the stove.

It is all so lovely, though I can never quite see myself among them. That does not stop me from trying.

Now that it is once more possible to leave this place for the first time since October, I do not believe I have the strength. I spend effort writing these words, but this is easier than grubbing for food. I found a clot of roots that tasted awful. I could not keep them down.

As the snow melts, more of Bib's and Bub's carcasses become exposed. I snapped some of the ribs and dug out whatever marrow I could from inside. As to the rest, there is little left save for a few clumps of hair. Even the hides have been dragged off somewhere. The wolves and other critters left little for me.

As in September, I am once more uncertain about what to do. Leave this place, walk toward Oregon, foraging as I go? Stay here, in the only place I know? It seems I have not changed much since September. I still cannot make up my mind.

MARCH OR APRIL, 1850

There are two pinches of cornmeal left in the sack. Then I am done.

APRIL, 1850

It has been nearly a week since I wrote in these pages. I had expected to be dead by now, but something happened.

The day after I last wrote, I was sitting on the wagon seat, as has been my custom. I held the shard of teacup to my nose and closed my eyes. I pretended I was once again back with my family, all well and alive and smiling. I still could not see myself among them.

I do not know how long I sat with my eyes closed, but a slight, far-off sound startled me. I opened my eyes and the sudden light made me blink. Everything was fuzzy. I heard that soft noise again, and squinted. Deer, I thought, eyeing the rolling land. And me with no way to kill them, nor fire to roast them. But it was not deer.

I held up a hand like a hat brim over my eyes and saw several people on horseback.

They saw me, I had no doubt, for they rode toward me. I suspected this was a trick of my mind. Then I knew it was, for the riders disappeared from sight. It was not until they reappeared, closer, slowly rising from the earth, that I realized they had walked down a dip in the valley floor, then up out of it again.

They took several minutes to reach me and I waited to see how long it would be before they disappeared for good. My long hair blew every way over my hand and face.

Perhaps it was Papa and the boys. That was the first time in ages I thought of them as still alive. Yes, I reasoned, that is it, they had gotten turned around and had to wait until spring to search for me. But then the riders drew closer and I saw they were Indians. Five of them.

I watched them. They were ten feet away when they stopped.

They were not real. They stared at me. One horse snorted and stamped a foot. Another shook its head. Still the men stared at me. I felt certain that as soon as I breathed or moved my hand from my eyes they would vanish.

The closest spoke.

"You here . . ." He held up his hands, spread them apart as wide as his chest. "Long time?"

Even hearing his voice, I knew he was not real. I kept looking at him, at the rest of them. Of the five, four led packhorses laden with animal skins and blanket-wrapped bundles tied with rope.

"You speak?" Again he held up a hand, this time at his mouth, moved his brown fingers away from his lips as if blowing seeds from a dandelion flower.

I nodded, though there was no one there.

He looked at the others, then back to me. They spoke low and quickly amongst themselves, words I had never heard. They looked around this infernal valley, pointed at the bones of Bub and Bib, nodded toward the wagon, all that was left of my family's journey.

Then they stopped talking and looked at me again. The man who had spoken slid down from his horse. There was no saddle, but a red-and-black-striped blanket that stayed in place.

He looked at me, motioned to a bare patch of dirt by his feet, on which he wore handsome moccasins. He crouched down, poking a finger, making a circle in the dirt. "We now." He motioned around him, at the valley. "We go." His finger dragged toward the west, leaving a ragged line. "Trade at fort of white

226

man." He stood, his hand rose up toward the mountains, then down again. He did this twice, three times, moving his hand like a slow-hopping rabbit.

"Long journey, many moon." He nodded at me. "You come. You white, you go there. No stay here," he said, shaking his head as if the thought of it was wrong to him. He looked once more at me, at the wagon, the stumps of trees I had chopped. "No more days."

Only then did I lower my hand. Maybe they were real people after all. I was not certain how to feel. I looked down at the bit of Mama's teacup in my dirty, scarred hands, at the one finger that froze some months back, and no longer moves. At my stained dress, once of a tiny red flower pattern, at my rag-wrapped feet I hadn't looked at in a month or more.

I suppose I should have cried. It was a long time before I looked up again, certain they would have vanished. But they were still there, watching me.

I opened my mouth, but nothing happened. I licked my lips, and tried again. "I . . . am Janette. Janette Riker."

APRIL, 1850

They made camp that night, and it took coaxing before I finally climbed down from the wagon. The one who spoke English held up a hand to help. I hesitated. How long had it been since I had touched another person? Since that morning when Papa hugged me before he left. I put my hand in that man's, and my breath caught short. He did not exactly smile with his mouth, but his eyes did. Kind eyes.

They shared food, good, hot, cooked food, venison and nuts and berries, the sweetness hurt my mouth. He told me to eat but a little. I wanted all of their food and then some. You will be sick he said, patting his belly. I did not want to hear that, but he was right.

APRIL, 1850

They are very kind to me and have shifted their load so I might ride on a packhorse. The route we are taking is a pretty one and I can't help but think Papa and the boys would have marveled at its beauty.

I pay careful attention to every tree, every rock, every sound the Indians make, the way the horses walk on the trail, all of it. Much of the time I spend convincing myself I have lived.

The morning after they found me we rode from the valley. I did not look back until it was almost too late. The wagon stood as always, so sad and alone. I tried to picture myself in it, but could not.

As we rode between a cleft in the great rock walls, I glanced once toward that southwesterly ridge, a folly on my part. There was no long-legged man with wispy gray hair and big hands, striding forward and smiling. He was not followed by two younger likenesses of himself, shoving one another and rushing to keep up. They were not shouting and waving to me, and never will again.

I would give anything to know what it was Thomas shouted to me that day from the ridge, the last words spoken to me by any of them. That abiding vision has stayed with me. Some might call it a memory best forgotten. I choose to think otherwise.

One day I will find them, my family, in a pretty green Oregon valley, tending a fine little farm. I will join them there, and we will have ourselves a grand time.

Soon, my little mountain valley pinched from my sight. I turned and faced west.

APRIL, 1850

We have been on the trail for nearly a week. The Indians are kindly toward me, though seldom speak. Parts of my body still pain me, my cut leg (though it is healing), my frostbit right ear, and various toes and fingers. If these are my worst woes, I count myself fortunate.

Last night at the campfire, as is my custom, I wrote in this diary. The man who speaks English, though I do not know his name, I think of him as Kind Eyes, watched me writing and motioned toward my diary. I could not bear the thought that someone else might hold this dear little book, a gift from both Mama and Papa. I closed it and held it tight to my chest, my eyes wide and staring at him.

He held up his hands, palms toward me. "No take," he said, but looked at the diary once more. Then he unrolled a skin-wrapped bundle and held up a small, beaded sack. He slid his hand in, then out, pointed at the diary, then at the pretty sack. He handed it to me and nodded. It was a gift.

I touched it, so very pretty in the firelight, the tiny beads all colors, and in a pattern like flowers. I am afraid I cried. He looked worried.

"Thank you." It was all I could think to say. I am a foolish girl. Such a fine and pretty gift and all I can do is cry and say thank you.

Kind Eyes smiled with his eyes and nodded, then sat down once more with his friends. They were quiet, and did not look at me as I sat there weeping and holding the pretty gift. This weeping is annoying, but I cannot control it.

I vow if anyone in my presence ever refers to Indians as "red savages," I will clout them.

November 12, 1850

It has been six months since I wrote in this, my dear little diary. And as there are few blank pages left, I fear my entries will be even sparser in future.

As to what has happened since I last wrote, I will endeavor to fill the gap with words.

It took us several weeks to reach the white man's settlement called Fort Nez Percés. It is operated by the famous Hudson's Bay Company, and is a bustling center for fur trade here in Oregon Territory, along the Columbia River.

On our arrival, I recall whispering, "So this is the land of milk and honey so many people yearn to see." I find my taste for milk and honey has soured.

I waved to the Indians as they left later the same day we arrived. At the last moment, Kind Eyes turned and nodded once, smiling with his eyes as he had before. It was enough. I will never forget him.

Shortly after my arrival I was taken in by a widow with three children. Mrs. Albemarle is a forthright woman who proposed an agreement with me. Once I regained good health she wished to hire me to assist in educating her offspring and keeping them out of mischief (largely the latter, I soon found). In exchange I would receive room and board. I agreed and it has been an amicable arrangement. The children are a challenge and remind me of Thomas. Needless to say I am busy.

I am told the Indians who found me are of the Salish tribe,

though I do not know if my spelling is correct. I also learned they found me at the end of the month of April. That made seven months I was alone. I find it curious that I prefer to keep company with my own thoughts these days, though I have had no urge to write in a diary. I also have not gained much in the way of weight. I eat enough to function, and leave the table thinking I could do with more. I do not care to dwell on the reason behind it.

All in all, I am as I once was, though I do walk with a limp, much as I try otherwise. It seems frost damaged two toes on my right foot such that I cannot feel them. It is the same with my dead finger. I massage it and no matter my efforts, it will not revive.

A doctor who passed through on a wagon train in June examined my hand, my leg, and my feet and told me I should count myself lucky, for any worse and the finger and those toes would have required amputation. I cannot abide that thought. I did lose part of my left ear to the cold, though as I can still hear out of it, it is of little consequence.

I will turn sixteen years of age in ten days. I do not know how I feel about that. I should consider it a boon, given that I never imagined surviving to see another birthday.

The summer and autumn have been busy here at the fort, with increasing numbers of travelers passing through, their countenances weary but relieved to have come this far. I cannot help but regard each person's face, listen in on every bit of conversation I am able, knowing it is a fool's errand. My family is gone and will not come back to me.

These fresh faces have largely blurred together in my mind. They roll in, resupply to suit their needs, then venture onward once more to lives of promise and hope in the land they longed to see, the unseen place of their heart's desire.

Not but a month ago, in early October, two ragged, late-season wagons arrived, all the way from Ohio. Among the company was a young man named Johan Sorenson. He was taken in as an orphan and raised as a farmhand. As soon as he was of age, he bid goodbye to all he knew and joined a wagon train bound for the west.

He is tall and strong, with messy hair the color of sun on ripe wheat in a field. His blue eyes spark and dance when he speaks of his future.

We have talked and walked for weeks now. In truth, Johan does most of the talking. In spring, he will settle a claim for 160 acres of good land. His conviction is hypnotizing and I find myself nodding and nearly smiling, so excited does he become about his plans.

Then he will stop so suddenly I have to look at him to make sure he has not bitten off his tongue. He reddens, and asks me some polite question about myself. I wish he would not.

I find it difficult to go on at length about much of anything. But I have begun to talk, to tell him of Mama, Papa, William, and Thomas. Yesterday I told him I lost them on our trip out here. Johan did not seem surprised. I suspect some chatty soul at the fort told him my story, what little they know of it, anyway.

I chanced a look at him, and he at me. Then he gripped my hand in his, gave it a squeeze, and did not let go.

EPILOGUE

Janey Pendergast closed the tatty old diary and sat with it on her lap. The attic had grown cold and dark beyond the oil lamp's low flame, now nearly out. No wind gusted the house, no rain pelted down. The storm had passed. Through the window she saw night had come.

"Oh no!" She stiffened and stood, clutching the diary to her chest. "No, no, no!" Janey grabbed the lamp and rushed down the stairs, nearly tripping twice. The entire short journey she kept thinking, I've ignored her all day. Mama is right. I am selfish, so selfish.

She halted outside the old woman's room. It was dark, cold, and quiet. Janey whispered, "Grandmother?" She heard no reply.

She crept in, set the dim lamp on a low table, and laid the diary on the bed. The old woman was there, as Janey had left her so many hours before. Not daring to breathe, Janey reached for the thin hand, felt it beneath hers. It was as cold as stone.

The sudden horrible weight of what she had done dropped on Janey. She had neglected her great-grandmother, and now because of Janey, this woman, this amazing woman, was dead.

She buried her face in the quilt, knotting it in her fists. "Oh, God, please forgive me, I am so sorry. I didn't mean it."

She felt a soft hand lightly stroke her hair.

"You read it, then."

Janey sat up. "You're alive! Oh, Grandmother, I am sorry, so sorry for earlier . . . all day."

"Hush now," said the old woman. "I am fine. I am old, old as sin,

but I am fine." She took the weeping girl's hands in hers. "The question is, are you?"

"I . . ." The girl looked down, her voice quiet. "I read it. Your secret diary."

"Good. I hoped you would." The old woman ran a finger along the book's worn cover, the edge of the crumpled beaded bag beneath.

Neither spoke for a few moments, then the old woman said, "I am sorry about your father, Janey. Losing him is something you will carry always." The old woman reached, slid open the drawer of her bedside stand. Her long fingers rustled inside, then stopped. "Hold out your hand."

Janey did and the old woman put something in her palm.

When Janey looked, she saw a shard of pottery, and jutting from it the delicate loop of a teacup handle decorated with tiny blue flowers.

"For when you miss him the most."

Janey looked at her great-grandmother and closed her eyes and held the little shard close to her nose. She breathed deeply and smiled.

They both did.

HISTORICAL NOTE: THE REAL JANETTE RIKER

Though *Stranded* is a novel of historical fiction, there really was a young woman named Janette Riker. Very little is known of her life, save for a few brief paragraphs in a book from 1877, *Woman on the American Frontier,* by William W. Fowler. In it, we learn that in 1849, Miss Janette Riker, age unknown, traveled from an unknown location toward Oregon Territory with her father and two brothers (names and ages unknown).

The family made it to the foot of the Rockies in late September, and rested in a little grassed valley in present-day Montana, intending to stay but two or three days. On the second day following their arrival, Miss Riker's father and two brothers left camp early to hunt buffalo. They never returned.

Janette waited too long for them, and early snows trapped her in the little valley. Struggling to push aside her growing despair, she built a crude shelter and killed and butchered their fattest ox, preserving the meat to the best of her ability. The harrowing winter brought repeated attempts by mountain lions and wolves to dislodge and devour her. In April, spring flooding wiped out her shelter and she nearly drowned.

Later that month an Indian hunting party found Janette, according to Fowler, in "the last stages of exhaustion," down to her last handfuls of soggy cornmeal and rancid meat. So moved were the Indians by this bedraggled but bold young woman, they fed her, loaded her few possessions on a horse, and escorted her to "Walla Walla station," likely the Hudson's Bay

Company trading post, called Fort Nez Percés, near the mouth of the Walla Walla River, in present-day Wallula, Washington.

Fowler mentions that Janette Riker eventually married a fellow emigrant (name unknown), and settled down to homestead and raise a family. Of her father and two brothers, no trace was ever found. It is assumed they were attacked and killed by hostile Indians, perhaps fell to their deaths, or somehow became lost in the vastness of the Northern Rockies.

I first came across mention of Miss Riker while researching a nonfiction book I wrote, *Cowboys, Mountain Men & Grizzly Bears: Fifty of the Grittiest Moments in the History of the Wild West* (2009). Though I devoted a brief chapter to her in that book, Janette's story stayed with me. In the years since, I asked myself, "What if . . . ? What if Janette Riker had kept a journal during that harrowing, formative winter? What if it were found many years later? By whom?"

These and many other questions led me to explore, in novel form, the possibilities and probabilities of Miss Riker's ordeal. In relating her story, I have used authorial license in fabricating, based on historical facts, a raw winter in the Northern Rockies as it may have been lived by a young woman, alone, in 1849 and 1850. Care was taken to ensure details about clothing, food, tools, and gear, as well as the terrain, flora, and fauna are as accurate as possible.

The resulting story is as much a paean to Janette Riker as it is an homage to those early emigrants who settled the western United States. I am humbled by their blind trust in the belief that what they were seeking would prove better than what they left behind. Often it did, though sometimes intrepid travelers never made it to their intended destinations, instead becoming casualties of the indifferent wilderness through which they trekked. I wonder about those who never made it, forever silent, their stories lost in the still-wild places of the West.

My wife and I, avid travelers, regard Miss Riker's incredible saga as inspiration to explore the lives and routes of westward emigrants of the nineteenth century. We find the past speaks volumes to those who take time to listen. And so, with ears perked, we search for clues to the life of the mysterious and courageous Janette Riker, who with fortitude and courage endured incredible hardship in the face of certain death . . . and survived.

—Matthew P. Mayo

ABOUT THE AUTHOR

Matthew P. Mayo is an award-winning author of thirty books and dozens of short stories. His novel, *Tucker's Reckoning*, won the Western Writers of America's Spur Award for Best Western Novel, and his short stories have been Spur Award and Peacemaker Award finalists. His many novels include *The Outfit: To Hell and Back; North of Forsaken; Winters' War; Wrong Town; Hot Lead, Cold Heart; The Hunted; Shotgun Charlie;* and others.

Matthew's numerous nonfiction books include the best-selling *Cowboys, Mountain Men & Grizzly Bears; Haunted Old West; Jerks in New England History;* and *Hornswogglers, Fourflushers & Snake-Oil Salesmen.* He has been an on-screen expert for a popular BBC-TV series about lost treasure in the American West, and has had three books optioned for film.

Matthew and his wife, photographer Jennifer Smith-Mayo, run Gritty Press (www.GrittyPress.com) and rove the byways of North America in search of hot coffee, tasty whiskey, and high adventure. For more information, drop by Matthew's Web site at www.MatthewMayo.com.

The employees of Five Star Publishing hope you have enjoyed this book.

Our Five Star novels explore little-known chapters from America's history, stories told from unique perspectives that will entertain a broad range of readers.

Other Five Star books are available at your local library, bookstore, all major book distributors, and directly from Five Star/Gale.

Connect with Five Star Publishing

Visit us on Facebook:
  https://www.facebook.com/FiveStarCengage

Email:
  FiveStar@cengage.com

For information about titles and placing orders:
  (800) 223-1244
  gale.orders@cengage.com

To share your comments, write to us:
  Five Star Publishing
  Attn: Publisher
  10 Water St., Suite 310
  Waterville, ME 04901